The
Hemlock
Anthology

Volume One

THE HEMLOCK ANTHOLOGY

VOLUME ONE

Edited by Shazia Parveen

THE HEMLOCK: A LITERARY ARTS JOURNAL

Lighted Lake Press

The Hemlock Anthology is a project of the online journal *The Hemlock: A Literary Arts Journal*. This volume is being published by Lighted Lake Press in coordination with *The Hemlock*.

ISBN 978-0-9969627-4-2 (paperback)
ISBN 978-0-9969627-5-9 (epub)

Library of Congress Control Number: 2024914455

Lighted Lake Press
Topeka, Kansas, USA
www.lightedlakepress.com

The Hemlock: A Literary Arts Journal
thehemlockjournal.org

INTRODUCTION

The Hemlock Anthology *is the first-ever anthology by* **The Hemlock: A Literary Arts Journal**. *It's a celebration of the diverse voices and creative expressions that unite us across borders and cultures. Within these pages, you will embark on a journey through the vivid landscapes of poetry and prose, and visual art on the covers, crafted by talented individuals from every corner of the globe.*

This anthology is a testament to the power of storytelling and the enduring human need to connect, to share our experiences, dreams, and visions. It is a mosaic of voices, each one distinct yet resonating with the universal themes that bind us together as a global community.

From the bustling streets of metropolises to the quiet serenity of rural landscapes, from the depths of personal introspection to the heights of collective imagination, the works contained herein traverse a vast spectrum of emotions, ideas, and perspectives. They invite us to explore the complexities of the human experience, to empathize with the struggles and triumphs of others, and to find beauty in the tapestry of life itself.

In this anthology, you will encounter poets who weave words into exquisite tapestries of emotion, and writers who spin tales that transport us to realms beyond our imagination. Each contribution is a testament to the boundless creativity that flourishes within the human spirit, transcending geographical boundaries and cultural divides.

We are honored to have you join us on this voyage of discovery and exploration, and we look forward to sharing many more adventures with you in the years to come.

~The Hemlock

TABLE OF CONTENTS

Two Worlds

By Antje Bothin

Living in two worlds
Can be challenging but really cool
Two countries I got to know
And two faces of Situational Mutism

One, quiet and invisible
Unseen, unheard in public
The other, loud and chatty
A confident leader at home

The world of black, red and gold
Struggles with humour and joy
The world of royalty, shepherd's pie and tea

So polite and nice, who would not stay

Living in two worlds
Can be enlightening and really great

It opens the window to new opportunities
So freedom can say hello

~~~
~~~

AI Is a Poet, I Am a Human

By Christopher Arkwright

The door is big.
Now tell me your emotions.
Do you feel dominated
By the weight of opportunities?
Does it remind you of a church
And ignite a religious fervour in your soul?

Now what if I told you
The door is just big.
And that's it.
Do you feel angry?
Do you want more?
Ok.
The door is also long.

You seem to be screaming.
It seems you want more.
Fine, it's red.

Now you are happy.
For a moment.
Basking in the satisfaction of
Identifying colour imagery.

But it doesn't mean anything
You tell me.

I tell you it does
I am an AI and I tell you
It is a commentary
On the nature of poems
Some incredibly intelligent references
To critics later,
You still tell me.

No.

That it is not poetry.

And I ask,
Aren't you the one
Who died a million times
For freedom of expression?

Aren't you the human?


~~~
~~~

Angels with Pencils

By Angela Townsend

I always thought poets were a higher life form.

This is likely because my mother is one, and she is the closest thing I have seen to a seraph on this heavy earth.

She is one in many millions, a liquid storyteller who spins gold from syntax. She can spell a memory in letters that feel like a mail from home, smuggling meaning into beauty. She will make you laugh and make you praise and make you remember you are not alone.

She will always make me want to be a better writer.

From my first poetic infatuations, play-dates with Emily Dickinson and Rumi, I knew I was no poet. I am an unsteady stack of pancakes beside their *petits fours*. I am the essay in excess, undisciplined flapping beneath their balloons.

Poetry breathes life into me, vital infusions against the hammering day. It is much easier to ply my petulant trade or scoop the litter box, clip coupons for pickles or pluck my eyebrows, so long as my lungs are light with Mary Oliver and David Whyte, Brian Doyle and Mom.

The very title of the magazine *Poets and Writers* implies two different species, silk swans vs. ducklings in dungarees. I am at peace with my place in this cosmology, grateful just to be in the pond.

But I have stubborn friends who see seraphs splashing in the sludge.

There is May, an octogenarian who responds to my emails with exclamation points punctuated by words. I tell her I'm praying for her, and she proclaims my patter poetry. I shoot Facebook messages reminding her she's radiant, and she insists they are newborn stars. We snap God-moments back and forth from the album of the mundane, and she prints my mushy missives. "Poetry!"

I scold May: "I'm blithering."

"Poetry!"

There is Priya, avid reader of my organization's newsletter, who lives behind kind lenses. Her rose haze likely translates the back of the Cap'n Crunch box into sonnets. She is kind and delusional: "Your writing is music."

I scold Priya: "That was an article about litter box maintenance."

"Everything can be music."

There is Stella, stubborn, a poetry glutton. She inspects my Instagram posts, exhuming individual flecks of glitter from the graveyard of the inane. She shares my slobbering with serious seraphs, reporting back with smugness: "Therese says you are a visual poet."

I scold Stella: "It's an Instagram caption."

"It's a gift to the world."

I suppose that is what I'm after. If writing is the one thing I'm sure I'm meant to do — writing and loving, which overlap in a full lunar eclipse in my case — I want to make it an offering.

I suppose I approach my email and my Instagram, my litter literature and my letters, like fireflies. They are small and ubiquitous, common as clover. But if they can cast a little light, I will line up jars as long as there are nights.

I know I'm no poet, no master artisan like my mother. I am an essayist at best, a vomit comet at worst. My writing is humid and unkempt, overgrown and under-crafted.

But I can't dispute that everything should be music.

I can't stop doing the one thing I'm sure I'm meant to do.

And I can't think of a better definition for poetry than gift.

~~~
~~~

How Can a Person Be Gold?

By Eman Mansoor

How can a person be like gold,
When they are mere flesh and bone?
How can poetry be so beautiful,
When it is composed of mere rhymes and words?
Love seems like a fantasy,
A curse no less than a crime,
That often breeds hatred and misery.

Everything in life is uncertain,
Even "forever" is just a word,
Bittersweet like caramel,
Compelling us to decorate our "future" together.

Meeting you was nothing short of a stroke of luck,
Making my wishes come true in a year of bad luck.
Now, as the days bid us farewell,
A new year awaits us.

So, my love, let us wish together,
That our bond may last forever.

~~~
~~~

Bored American, Once-Visitor to Relatives' Western Galilee GesherHaZiv Kibbutz near Northern Border, Kibitzes

By Gerard Sarnat

I fell into a burning ring of fire
Went down, down, down
And the flames went higher
And it burns, burns, burns
The ring of fire
The ring of fire

--Johnny Cash, "Ring of Fire"

Let each of us Jews now blow the shofar…

They* say Tehran's not engaging in an all-out war
Because Iran is not yet a nuclear threshold power
+ gossip Supreme Leader's pissed Hamas' boss
Didn't forewarn them of their October 7 attack
& since "fire of fire" deployments're on-going
With Syria's potentially ur-massive missile
Infrastructure slowed-down by our Israel
With G-d's help oy vey iz mir so far!

But nevertheless there's great chance
I.D.F. will strike first into Lebanon
Given currently *Unique conditions*
Unlikely to return: social cohesion
Support from the U.S.A. [sic?]
Solidarity with world's Jewry
[ditto?] -----and international
Legitimacy [in whose dreams]

...You Israelis really do want that ------ or rather prefer these

sweetheart deal schemers shall be superseded by wiser people?

*ASTARTA (אתחלתא), 16November2023

~~~
~~~

Unveiling the Past: Returning to the Land of Peacocks

By Ruchi Acharya

After a decade spent abroad, where I subsisted mainly on salads, I found myself back in India, the land of peacocks. It was a momentous return, brimming with an unforgettable collection of memories from a different life and insightful experiences. I vividly recall a spring day in Hawaii, enjoying a Vodka Martini with a hint of lemon peel in the company of my beloved. Suddenly, the ring of my phone shattered the tranquility, delivering the devastating news of my mother's passing. In an instant, my world crumbled, and I was consumed by an overwhelming sense of grief and despair.

I returned to my hometown to partake in the somber funeral ceremony, giving condolences to my mother. Regrettably, it was too late to convey anything. All the aspirations, dreams, and yearnings to be with my mother had been reduced to nothingness. In Hinduism, we believe that the soul resides in the physical vessel for so long that it hesitates to depart when a person passes away. Therefore, to release the soul, we burn the body upon the funeral pyre.

In the days following the funeral, I found myself drawn to my mother's bedroom, exploring the remnants of her final days. I ventured into her peaceful cupboard, where I found some placid clothes neatly ironed and folded within the wardrobe. As I wandered, my eyes fell upon an unfinished half-knitted scarf, a vibrant red nail polish, and a collection of handwritten recipes resting on her bedside drawer. And in the Pooja room, adorned with her skillfully crafted paintings, the walls bloomed with Swastika and Om symbols, showcasing her artistic devotion.

In the living room, I noticed my childhood photo album left open on the lounge chair, inviting memories to flood my mind. Memories surged forth, urging me to delve into the unexplored and long-forgotten days of my life. With a sense of anticipation, I settled onto the chair and began my nostalgic journey.

The first photograph greeted me with an image of me as a baby, innocently sucking my toes, completely unclothed. Upon closer examination, I noticed a small black dot adorning my cheeks. It wasn't a birthmark but rather the protective mark of kajal (also known as Kohl), applied by my mother to ward off the evil eye. It fascinated me, bringing a smile to my face as I realized how deeply she cared for me.

Turning the page, I encountered a snapshot of my five-year-old self, eagerly assisting my mother in preparing the lip-smacking ladoos (a sweet dish) for the festival of lights, Diwali. In the photograph, I saw my small, imperfectly shaped ladoos placed beside my mother's perfectly round creations. It evoked a smile, reminding me of the joyous moments shared in the kitchen.

Flipping to the next page, my heart skipped a beat as I beheld an image of myself draped in a saree. I vividly remembered how my mother skillfully adorned me in one of her favorite sarees for a cultural event. She embellished me with bangles and placed a crimson tikka on my forehead, ensuring I exuded an authentic ethnic charm. What a sport she was. I remember she was always an active participant in all of my school functions, and her love and support knew no boundaries. Words fail to express the depth of my regret for not being there with her in her final days. With a heavy sigh, I reluctantly turned to the next page, my heart weighed down by sorrow.

There, I found myself captured with a fishtail braid. Memories flooded back of the meticulous efforts my mother put into crafting this unique hairstyle every single day during my school years. The photograph depicted me in my school uniform, proudly displaying the fishtail braid. Tears welled up in my eyes as I grieved the absence of her nurturing presence. With a heavy heart, I somberly flipped through the remaining pages of the album, each image a poignant reminder of the love and care my mother bestowed upon me.

After relishing the golden memories of my happy childhood, I contemplated the term "lineage" while sipping herbal tea on an Indian swing in the balcony. I pondered on the importance of passing down our Indian rituals and traditions to my own children. Yet, a twinge of uncertainty crept in as I considered how these practices might be perceived as peculiar by people in foreign lands. I questioned how I could ensure the continuation of my lineage for future generations while navigating the intricacies of cultural integration abroad.

I made a bold decision that I would not allow the delicate Indian lineage of my ancestors to fade away. It became clear to me that I wanted to preserve their existence in the smallest details of my everyday life, starting with serving traditional dishes for breakfast such as Dhokla, Upma, and Poha. I can bet the aroma of these dishes will knock you off from the table. With this determination, I extended my stay at my parents' home for the following month.

Embarking on my journey to discover and understand my history, I began by conversing with my parents' relatives, friends, and neighbors. Upon queries, I got to know more about the charities and cultural communities they used to visit every weekend. Through these conversations, I collected invaluable information about their way of life, traditions, and experiences. It was a delightful and enlightening process, as I discovered the rich tapestry of stories and memories that shaped my family's heritage. I recognized that this was the most fitting way to honor the memory of my dear departed mother.

In addition, I dedicated a week to document my family history. I delved into the local library and museums, unearthing hidden treasures of knowledge. The tales of our ancestral struggles and the remarkable progress we have achieved astonished me. Each of these tribal symbols carries distinct meanings, embodying both simplicity and a challenge to the modern way of life. I gained profound insights into the importance of practicing traditions, celebrating festivals, speaking our native language, and actively engaging with our community.

The most fascinating tale of all was the Hindu epic tale of Ramayana. Instantly, I wanted to know the very reason why Diwali is such an auspicious festival for Hindus. The legend unfolds to the Prince Rama, an incarnation of the god Vishnu, and his extraordinary journey. Rama was born as the eldest son of King Dasharatha; he got exiled to the forest for fourteen years due to a twist of fate. Accompanied by his devoted wife Sita and unwavering brother Lakshmana, Rama faces numerous challenges during their exile, including the abduction of Sita by the demon king Ravana. With the help of a mighty monkey army led by Hanuman, Rama wages a great war against Ravana to rescue Sita and restore righteousness. The epic explores themes of honor, duty, loyalty, love, and the triumph of good over evil, making it a cherished story that continues to inspire people across generations.

My journey to get to know more about my history not only provided me with a deeper understanding of my lineage but also ignited a sense of pride and gratitude for the vibrant cornucopia of culture that flows through my veins. Armed with newfound knowledge and a renewed dedication, I felt empowered to preserve and pass down the legacy of my ancestors for my future generations to cherish.

Namaste


~~~
~~~

The Gutenberg Galaxy

By Ben Nardolilli

Building a machine at the start of morning,
part of a process of integrating myself
both horizontally and vertically into ingot, cog,
and widget, eventually management too,
though I doubt I could handle the marketing

With coffee and cafe space, I launch
the saved program for the syncretic rundown,
turning and binding inner wheels to release
a product packaged in line with current events,
after testing it against long-term trends

Desire and dread are cast into dies, codified
in order to make sure no madness
or dreams are wasted as words run together
on a belt that conveys a growing sense
as it rolls along to the end of each new stanza


~~~
~~~

Pliosaur Skull

By Christian Ward

"Colossal pliosaur sea monster skull on display in Dorset" - *BBC News*

Oversized talisman, cavernous getaway
for gulls and other seabirds. Look how you ward
away the warring rainclouds, thunder
beating its drum. Your teeth – a full armoury
of mussel-black weaponry – dulled like a memento from our future.

~~~
~~~

Permission

By Christopher Rubio-Goldsmith

Sometimes to love someone you need to be a stranger. Eyes full
of Mexican surreal poetry and hips feeling that Miles Davis trumpet.

I loved watching you poor the tequila into coffee cups
with superheroes near the handles. The limes sliced

and thrust into full lipped puckers. Who were we those
nights? If I knew the words, would I have spoken them?

Those cups empty. Lime rinds in the sink. The books
left open, a pen in the spine to save the place.

I wanted you to tell me all of your story. It always began
with you telling me your father loved Steve McQueen.

I could listen to you talk about the coffee shop or
a wild day throwing empty bottles into the dumpster.

How many chances did we use up? I gave myself
permission to be sad. (That was how long it lasted.)

And over the next several years we encountered each other
at the back door of a restaurant or walking on the mall

between classes. Me cupping the match trying
to light up a Camel. You holding a French book

or a poster board full of graphs and crooked lines.
Our hands too full for gestures. I wanted

you to know the words I was saying
in my head. They were rivers in spring.


~~~
~~~

Mutiny

By Clyde Liffey

Like most men of my age and station in life I awake every morning dreaming of chucking it all. Thinking these thoughts, I wasn't thinking those thoughts, I was watching the road, I didn't miss my exit, nevertheless instead of pulling into the office park I pulled into the nature preserve not a half mile away from my workplace. I backed into a spot in the empty lot, got out, remembered my briefcase was in the back. I beeped the car doors open, popped the trunk, put the briefcase inside. As I turned, my glasses were knocked off my face by a dangling branch. I picked them up. They weren't cracked, they needed a cleaning, there was no place to adequately clean them, this is not an emblem for how I see the world.

As I was examining my glasses a short spectacled woman wearing a polo shirt with the preserve's insignia approached me. "Are you a member?" she asked.

"No, I"

"It's OK," she said after examining my windshield. "Carry on." She turned and walked away to open the small office slash gift shop the society keeps there.

I watched her go then entered the trail area. The paths were both familiar and unfamiliar to me. Whenever I stick to the open well-marked trails I never get lost. I finish my walk timely and dissatisfied. Whenever I embark upon the more challenging so-called intermediate trails I invariably get lost. I stop at a height if there is a height, mark the position of the sun, and rue that I didn't do that before I started. I finish those walks late, scratched, and relieved that the jaunt wasn't worse than it could have been. This time I ignored the sun to inspect my brown oxford shoes which were already dusty. My pants, but enough about my clothes – time to be off!

A walk in the woods should clear your head, walks aren't magic. Of course, I thought of what I was shirking. My boss chose me to present our department's accomplishments to the company this morning. I'd spent the last week and a half writing and revising slides – making them shorter, punchier, more outlandish – while also performing my other assigned duties. Last night I came home and straight off roused my napping laptop. After ninety minutes or so I needed a break. The light outside was fading, we were within a week or so of the summer solstice. I took one of my usual routes, small danger of getting lost on suburban streets. A few minutes into my stroll, still coping with eye strain, I noticed the noble profile of a robin on a lawn. It didn't hop or fly away. It merely cocked its head and stared at me. Something in its expression reminded me of my father's grizzled visage. When I returned home still dizzy from the day, I splashed water on my face and gazed at my sparse mostly white whiskers.

Last night's walk was neither prelude nor parallel to this morning's.

"To your left," I heard and complied though my step wasn't lively.

She was probably older than the gift shop attendant though many would say she looked better. She wore tight black shorts and a sleeveless top. Her left arm was covered with monitors. Her breathing was hard, her body was hard, inviting and uninviting. She glanced at a display on her wrist, deftly dodged a protruding root in the trail, and was soon out of sight. I stumbled over that root or one of its offshoots, heard the high-pitched squeal of a hawk, I might have kept it from its prey. I reached for the tree, missed it, stayed nonetheless erect. A drop of sweat may have formed on my brow. I thought of the sweaty jogger with her hard and soft parts, her heavy breathing, her constant attention to herself, I came to the woods to get away from myself, to see the world plain like some vigilant lizard,

I wasn't sure why I was there. I reached in my pocket for a handkerchief, I didn't have one, would its whiteness be out of place here? I'd barely gone forty yards and was almost completely disoriented.

There was still time to get to work and present my slides. After a thirty-minute sabbatical he emerged from the wilderness and delivered a spot on demonstration. Everyone was wowed. Reflecting on his performance while munching on a delicious raspberry pastry he said

Anything of that sort is of course completely beyond me. I came to this town, I wasn't born far from here, I chose – chose! – to stay in the area. The animals at my feet, hidden now, have less of a choice, the caged ones even less, the dead ones:

Walking along

Die Self Die

& other constructs

I came to this trail, I don't know why I came here, by then I was further along for my legs took me as if by their own volition when I happened upon

"Good throw, Finn!"

Finn's mother turned to me as if urging me to cheer him on. I looked down at her for the path was about five feet above the bog where they were playing. She climbed up the embankment all the while watching her son. "He's a good boy," she said still looking up at me for she was small. "At first it was a big adjustment, short-circuiting my career to raise him, I never wanted a boy, I wanted girls, little ballerinas, my husband transferred to this area for the opportunity, it's paid off for him, me too since I don't need to work, I have time to fulfil other interests, volunteering for example, when I return to the workforce in a few years, after Finn is established in grade school, I'll"

"You remind me of someone," I said, for she looked like someone I knew in high school but how could that be, didn't she say where they were from, she rejoined her son, something in what I said or how I said it, the boy kept plunking rocks, I shrugged, more shrunk than shrugged, and turned away.

I sensed a scent I once knew well. The tallest boy, wearing a wool hat over his shaggy hair, dropped the butt and stamped on it. He swilled his beer, sneered at me. "I told you it was nobody," one of the others said.

"What are you doing here, old man?" the tall boy asked.

"I'm just taking a nature walk."

"Dressed like that?"

I stepped back, looked at my dress shoes. I was wearing my best khaki pants and my presentation blue shirt. "Nature inspires me," I said. "What are you doing here?"

"We live in this town. We belong here."

"Isn't this a school day?"

The two shortest boys pushed me against a tree. "It's graduation day, uncle. We're just having a little celebration before we put on our caps and gowns."

"That's right," the other said, "we're rebels. Do you have a problem with that?"

"Of course not," I said. "I was young"

The boy who was taking the few bills I kept in my wallet looked at me as though in disbelief. The tall boy flashed a knife. "You aren't going to say anything about this, are you?"

"Of course not. I'm playing hooky myself."

They gave me my wallet back, took the battery out of my phone. "Let grandpa go," the tall boy said. "He can reminisce about his wild and crazy youth for the rest of his nature walk."

Once I was a few yards beyond them one of the short boys ran up to me and put his hand on my shoulder. He gave me back my phone battery and a business card. "There's no phone service here," he said. "If you need any work done on your house, call this number. I'll get you a discount."

Head down, I thought of what they called me – uncle though I have no siblings, grandfather though I'm childless, not mister. I was young once, drank timorously from the cup, drained it partway and now

"I never expected to see you here," the gray-haired man on the bench said.

"I come here a lot."

"Not on Fridays, not on workdays."

"Who are you?"

"Don't you remember?" His tone wasn't sinister but not benevolent either.

I sat at the far end of the bench from him. The bench was on a small rise. It offered a prospect of a banal patch of woods. "You do look like"

"I am – in the flesh."

"How could that be? You died"

"Did you see the body?"

"I was too young."

"And I was too alive. We evacuated the plane well before we allowed it to crash in the mountainside. If there were bodies to be seen they'd have been overflowing with life! But enough about me, what"

"Enough about me," he said but I still wasn't sure who he was. My mother's father and older brother were near lookalikes to me when I was young. They operated a small farm before such things became the rage. On weekends I'd visit them. Then during the week I'd come home from school and pore over my picture books of animals, dreaming of becoming a naturalist the way other boys dreamed of becoming sports stars.

"I said"

"I heard you," I snapped.

He was eating almost soundlessly from a small box of crunchy cereal poached from some kindergartner's field trip backpack no doubt. "It's funny how you become attached to a place. You probably know that before the crash we were operating a drug farm, there wasn't much money in beets and such then. The heat was closing in, we had to fake our deaths. We went out West for a while where we wouldn't be known but within five years we had to come back. Been here ever since," he chuckled.

"But how"

"Didn't I say enough about me?"

"Of course I still love animals," I said thinking of all the pets I never had. "You spy on me here on weekends, you must realize that."

He folded up the cereal box he'd just finished, put it in his rucksack, extracted another. "We're not talking about me," he repeated.

"Do you want me to give a full accounting of myself?"

"You can tell me a little more than what I can gather from an occasional glimpse of you on a Sunday afternoon."

I put my now sweaty head in my hands, thought of reaching for my cell phone. I wondered what my relative would think of the wondrous technology at my fingertips. I remembered my old animal books – my mother threw them out once I started high school – how I'd contemplate that soft mammalian fur, dream of

I had a good head for math in those days. My father pushed me towards business school. I was young, I wanted to, another cousin was arrested for possession, I was scared or somehow put straight.

I turned to him. "I," I said, but he was gone.

I don't know how occasional fits of swagger overcome me. Perhaps I was buoyed by my conversation with my direct or indirect forebear. Whatever its cause, I rose from the bench and sauntered down the lane like the romantic lead in some postwar Italian movie.

If I had a sports coat, I'd have draped it over my shoulder. The dust on my shoes and the hems of my pants was fitting, part of my raffish charm. I was

"Again, to your left!"

I was swaying in the middle of the walkway. Her monitors still pulsing, sweating hardly more than she was when she first passed me, the jogger sniffed or snorted at my lack of progress. This time though we were on a plain: I could observe her more closely. Her black – no sign of gray – ponytail oscillated with a frequency as regular as her strides on the level ground. I imagined holding her, one hand on her bare muscular midriff, another lower down, she'd have to shower of course, I'm finicky that way. Just before a bend in the path she turned and stuck her tongue out at me. My self-regard evaporated. Head down I reached the bend a few minutes later.

"Marcello! Give me a hand with this."

I turned and saw Giancarlo lugging a cooler. I jogged over to him, grabbed one of the handles. Marcello and Giancarlo aren't our real names. We give ourselves fanciful tags to relieve the drudgery of our work lives. I wondered if I should have included that in my slides.

"I didn't expect to see you here," Giancarlo said as we approached the picnic tables.

"Nor I you," I said.

"The morning presentations were cancelled," he explained, "technical difficulties. HR asked for volunteers to help set up the company picnic and since I didn't have anything better to do, here I am." We placed the cooler in a shady spot, straightened up. "What's with the get up?"

Giancarlo was wearing shorts, sandals, and – what everyone else there had on – a Hawaiian shirt. The party – I was so focused on my presentation that I'd completely forgotten about it – wasn't themed so far as I knew.

I reached into the cooler, popped open a beer. One of the HR functionaries approached and took the can from me. "No drinking, and only in moderation of course, until the party starts. Besides, it's only 10 am. Go help the people setting up the tent."

I saw a group of men I don't know planting the center pole. "But I was helping Giancarlo."

She pursed her cherry-red lips. "Who's Giancarlo?"

He was already gone.

"We have these company get-togethers so people from different departments can get to know each other," she continued. She emptied the beer can. Some of the beer splattered on my shoes. "I can already write you up for inappropriate drinking. Go," but I was already walking away.

~~~
~~~

Yo, Picasso

By GTimothy Gordon

The highest walls melt before me.

-Picasso, photo caption of self-portrait, summer 1901-

Consider me at 20 in-heat, like Paris, black cloak, black hair,
black beard, black eyes, the aughts, sans francs, friends, tongue,
full of myself, dream and vision to expiate among othered Other
misérables in Montmartre, Montparnasse, known from my high
hovel-*atelier*, with Braque, *notre avenir dans l'air* gone-bust,
so solo I'd show the clucks what's what, set the century on fire,
deflate a past still preening, all-in with my genius before the lean-in,
copycat, cool-kid *isms*, consider my hands (so Stein says), delicate,
of a pianist, shape-shifter among splodgy French bric-a-brac art
spooked by all that's New and Now from the get-go by gendarmes,
government, for talking langue of art, *a mí,* alien, *métèque,* never
      artiste,
never metier, *never citizen,* surveilled, spied on by lowlife snitches,
given the French bureaucratic go-by time and again, despite my
      cosseted blues,
rosés that crush the canvas, often your heart, not just *La Vie, Les*
      Demoiselles,
Weeping Woman, Child with a Dove, the *Saltimbanques,* all Blind
      Minotaurs,

The Tragedy, Guernica, rejected by higher-ups, especially my spot-on
       Angles
more avant than Armory garde nudes descending, blues and toilets,
       when all
went surréaliste, after me, Dali céléb, even postwar Yank
       abstractionist
pretenders, thugs really, boozing it up in Bowery bars, but me, my
       mythic feel
even with brutalist touches, working overtime on what I was before
       becoming
what I am every moment, the dealers, collectors, money guys, who
       knew passion
and genius, always my worth, even with my synthetic paste-on
       "founds," readymades,
cash-money awash as I negotiated both wars, Olga and I hobnobbing
       upscale
Danse Russe artistes in pricey flats, Normandy château, trolling
       le pays, chauffeured
luxe Hispano-Suiza limo, new mistress in-hand, partying with
       Dominguín after the bulls,
even before PapáH! Remaking a smug, certain world, seeing it still
       fresh, accessible,
mysterious, just when everyone thought all was stable, safe, and
       absolute for a little while
before and after each calamity, until The Bomb, then deeper-in
       mining my god instinct,
creation *en-soi*, and what a joy it was, still is, working at what, even
       past ninety, is in flux,
for what else is there, rich or poor, young, old, scholar, scamp,
       but to find oneself

in the moment as at Gósol when all went dark with vision and
        voice, the who you think
you are, might be, ever seek, even for a microsecond before passing,
        the what I'm after,
my very being, Yo soy, sin arrogancia, ahora y *por* siempre,
        más grande que la vida,
Yo, Picasso


~~~
~~~

Sidewalk Café Rendezvous

By James Kangas

One shows up late, of course,
nervous, getting things
off on a wrong foot.
The other succumbs
to a reflexive pause.

The moon sails her silver arc
two days slimmer
since their reluctant goodbye,
and the night floats an impromptu cloak
shutting out that little magic.

A faint music bewilders their ears
and their eyes drift off
after passing strangers.
Conversation dwindles,
the candle untended.

None of this was intended.
None of it
was what they thought it might be
two days ago at first sight—
a little sketch begun

(the delicate perspective
now quite askew) in pencil, say,
or watercolor,
of two not quite completed people
leaning over a table.

~~~

First published in brix (Flint, MI), Spring, 1986
~~~

Safe Harbor

By DC Diamondopolous

The Catalina Express docked alongside the pier. The ride from Long Beach had been choppy as the boat bounced over swells; passengers stumbled on deck and spilled drinks while waves hammered the bow. I've traveled the channel every year since I can remember, but this was the first time to the island without my mother.

I lifted the backpack over my shoulder and walked down the ramp.

Six months since she passed. Mom continued to provoke me everyday, even in my dreams. The ebb and flow of her sanity centered on me.

I'd come to Catalina to film a tribute for my mother and post it on YouTube. A knot of anxiety and excitement coiled inside me.

I'd always been what others called "strange," with extremely large eyes, dark with a hint of sclera. Classmates had called me a grey, my hair, Crayola yellow. It couldn't be dyed: it didn't absorb peroxide and gave me an edge without wanting one. My skin was a rusted gold, as if I sunbathed on Mercury.

Boys would see me from a distance or from my back—my hair a natural curiosity—then, when they neared, or I turned around there would be an intake of breath, a fallen expression. It hurt to disappoint.

My oddness went beyond the visual. I felt people's emotions; if I hugged or touched them, the sum of their experience seeped into my being. The weirdest, the most fantastical of all, was that I smelled people's consciousness. I'd be at the farmers' market, shoppers intent on picking greens or fresh fruit, the odor pleasant, but when hostile music blasted from a car stopped in traffic, the shoppers' collective stench of anger filled me with nausea. Fear, the greatest stink, rose to unbearable heights. The world boiled with it.

I found refuge as the groundskeeper at the Self Realization Fellowship in the Pacific Palisades, where the atmosphere was serene, the tranquil lake where swans and mallards glided by, a perfect setting to reflect.

With the world's religions celebrated at my home, you'd think I'd be religious. I was devoted, joyous, when I dug my fingers into the earth, planted and pruned, fed the ducks and feral cats. My affection for animals and plants taught me to nurture an inner kind of beauty. Mother Earth, my religion.

Mom loved my strangeness. She hated it, too, lashing out, calling me my father's weirdo child. She was an artist, with a yoyo temperament, creamy-white skin and once in a while an eerie mannequin stare. Men chased her until they stumbled over her pile of baggage. Our home in Long Beach had wall-to-wall signed prints and paintings from Escher to Warhol, including her own work. Her water colors and prints sold in galleries. She was a renowned illustrator.

With her gone, the craving to discover who I am possessed me.

Every night for the past week I'd stir, throw off my covers, waken from a dream of my half-sister, Jemjasee. She too had enormous eyes and hair like mine. Mom called it, "Lichenstein yellow." In my dreams, Jemjasee stood at the Little Harbor overlook on the Conservancy side of Catalina where my mother took me, a ten-year-old, to meet my father and Jemjasee. I'd awake as if called, the dream, vivid, and I'd be on the precipice overlooking the Pacific, searching the sea just as my mother did when we'd go back every year to the island. She'd wait for my father, pace the cliffs, but he never appeared.

I searched the pier for Carlos.

He stepped from the dark terminal as light skipped across the ceiling slats. The night she passed, I called him; we talked, wept, laughed. Carlos cherished my mother like an older sister, and now that I saw him—his cowboy hat shading his crinkled face—his presence consoled me.

We stood, arms entwined holding each other. It would be vulgar to talk while closeness tallied our grief. I promised myself I would be the one to comfort and not the other way around. He trembled. I held tighter, loving him for loving my mother.

"Man, I thought you'd stay longer, Gwendolyn," he said, pulling away. His rugged face damp.

"I can't."

"Spend Thanksgiving with us. Stay the week."

"I'll let you know."

"You got the equipment?"

"It's in my backpack."

He put his tattooed arm around my shoulder, and we headed toward the terminal.

"Maria and the kids want to see you," he said, releasing me as we moved through the crowd.

"I have to be here at five."

"You'll have plenty time," he said as we came to his truck. "You have a speech or something?"

I shook my head.

"No notes?" He placed my bag in the bed of his Ford.

"Don't need them."

"It would help."

Carlos had played the role of wise uncle since I was a child.

He opened the passenger door. "Where you wanna go?"

"Upper Terrace first. I can get a great shot of Avalon."

His truck smelled of refried beans and coffee. It also carried the sweet tang of a man who loved his family and life on the island. But mixed in the smells, I caught whiffs of anxiety, perhaps about his future or Maria. The Ford caked with years of dust, grooved with dirt around the steering wheel. I rested my feet on a tool box and pondered my mother's story. She had talked in a cacophony of innuendos, ambiguous retorts, and said things to get a reaction so her sincerity was always in question. I wanted to know about my father and Jemjasee. What happened on that day overlooking Little Harbor when my mother ran to my father, threw herself into his arms? I'd never seen her so happy. He kissed my forehead. A gentle being that cooed in a sing-song accent as he stroked my hair, the same effulgence as his own. I watched my parents head down the trail and disappear.

Jemjasee took my hand, and we walked the bluffs. She asked me questions, "What did I like to do, could I swim, did I have many friends?" She spoke as an equal, even though she had to be a lot older. We danced, laughed and skipped, did cartwheels and played hand-clap games. I had so much fun with my sister that I forgot about my parents.

My mother returned sobbing. Jemjasee kissed me good-bye, and I'm not sure what happened next, but my father and sister vanished.

"Where did they go?" I had asked. "Why are you crying?"

My mother howled. It hurt my ears.

"I'm afraid to leave!" She screamed and pounded her fists on the side of her head until I grabbed her, not letting go until her wails turned to whimpers.

Through the years I'd bring up that day, and she'd snap, "Don't live in the past." Then five years ago, on my twenty-fifth birthday, I told her my wish was to know about my father and Jemjasee.

"They come from far away."

"Luke Skywalker far?" I said with sarcasm.

Tears welled in her eyes. She stared into her wineglass, then played a Joni Mitchell album. I regretted my ridicule. She hurt easily and never spoke of them again.

Carlos drove up the hill and parked along the turn-out.

"This is perfect," I said, pulling out the camera.

"I'll do it," Carlos said.

"Thanks, but I got it." I videoed everything in sight, including Carlos, the Art Deco Casino Ballroom, moored sailboats, The Express docked at the pier, the Glass Bottom Boat, past the harbor condos built into the mountain like a honeycomb. I aimed the camera at homes stacked above their view of Avalon Bay, and two tourists who drove by in a golf cart.

"Drop me off at Little Harbor overlook, will you?"

"Hey man, I thought I was gonna help you."

"It's something I need to do by myself. Give me three hours."

Carlos took off his cowboy hat, his rugged face brown as the hills. He smoothed back his dark graying hair.

"Two," he said. "Make time for Maria before your boat leaves."

"I planned on it."

I put the camera inside my bag in the back of the truck.

"Why Little Harbor?"

"Mom liked it."

"She never said anything to me about it. Man, she could be loopy." He laughed. "When she was at our house—before smart phones, you were a kid—she'd leave messages to herself on her answering machine. A diary type thing." He sniffed. "I never knew if she was for real or not."

"She talked in riddles."

"Man, she was a trip. Kindest person I ever knew." He opened the door and hopped into the driver's seat.

We drove up Divide Road, past the Wrigley residence, turned on Old Stage Road and headed into the interior.

We passed bison, their ancestors left in the olden days when they made cowboy movies. Carlos stepped on the gas. He drove up and over the drought ridden hills.

In minutes, we were at Airport-In-The-Sky. The three towers, Spanish tile, and wagon wheels with plants tangled through the spokes. Small, isolated, just like its name—in the sky.

Mom never shed her hippie beads and anklets, walking barefoot, doing yoga, and vegan diet. She told me she burned her bras in the seventies, slept with Jim Morrison, dropped acid and tried to be a lesbian. She also read movie magazines, had facials, manicures and wore make-up. She was a glamorous hippie. Until the day she passed, she burned incense, though the doctors told her not to, and played Carole King and Aretha Franklin albums.

She had me at the age of thirty-seven, said it was the best thing that ever happened to her.

Mom's last words were, "Gwendolyn, don't worry about the Earth. As soon as man destroys himself, the Earth will replenish."

Carlos drove along the dirt road beside the pine and eucalyptus trees.

Nothing had changed since that day twenty years ago—the pyramid-like cliffs, brown fields of brush and cacti, blue and white everywhere, the sky, the sea, wisps of clouds, and ribbons of breakers crashing against the rocks.

Carlos went off-road and parked at the overlook.

"Two hours." I opened the door, went to the flatbed, unzipped my backpack, pulled out the tripod and camera and dropped the bag on the ground.

Carlos slammed the door. "Need help?"

"I got it."

He looked at the mountains. "Man, we could sure use some rain." He sighed. "Be back at three, then we go see Maria."

The truck wheels kicked up dirt. He made a sharp turn and drove off.

I adjusted the tripod, clamped on the camera, highlighted the settings.

Looking into the lens, I said, "I'm the daughter of Megan Jones, an artist, who grew up in the 1960s. You've probably seen her work, especially if you read romance novels. But her landscape water colors also—." Flashes appeared in the lens. "Ah, what now?" Was I out of focus? My settings off? It had a six-hour battery life. In the lens, I saw a starburst break above me, a shower of fallen rays. I spun around. Beams of light pranced above the ocean. They skipped, danced. I moved to the precipice. Riveted by the lights, I watched as particles rearranged themselves, silver, glittered. I stepped to the rim of the bluff, laughing, as if the spectacle were for me. The lights disappeared.

Dejected, I waited, stared out to sea, searched the sky, no airplanes or helicopters. What was it? Mystified, I turned to the camera.

There it was!

Molecules rearranged themselves, several hundred feet across the field. The mirage shimmied without form. I aimed the camera when a portal of light appeared. The person in the arch I knew to be Jemjasee.

I ran, gulping air. Tears, laughter, questions and sorrows erased. I felt my mother beside me. Was it her voice or my imagination? "Yes, Gwendolyn, part of you does come from far away."

Jemjasee floated down a ramp that extended before each step, elegant in a kaleidoscopic jumpsuit, her lithe figure youthful, yellow hair, golden bronze skin.

I slumped into her arms. Her love radiated on everything, the purple blooming cacti, the brown chaparral turned brilliant with color, her consciousness a fragrance of a thousand bouquets.

"Father?"

She shook her head and took a necklace with a pendant that hung around her neck.

"He made it for you, should I ever see you again."

"What is it?"

"A red diamond with Catalina quartz that he excavated a long time ago. The diamond is from my home, Seren."

"It's gorgeous. Thank you," I said, putting it over my head. "I dreamt of you."

"And you came."

"Why couldn't we have been a family?"

"On Seren, anyone with the V-Gene is forbidden to immigrate. Father wanted to settle somewhere else, but your mother was afraid of leaving here."

I'm afraid to leave. Now her ravings made sense.

"What's the V-gene?"

"The gene of violence."

"Why couldn't we all live here?"

Jemjasee shook her head. "It would be like drowning, for Father and me, if we lived on Dual."

"Dual?"

"That's what we call Earth. Everything here is either good or bad, rich or poor, win or lose. The pendulum swings, happy one moment sad the next. That's why we call Earthlings 'Dualities.'" She touched my face, a breeze against my cheek. "On Seren, we don't live in the outer so much as the inner world."

"All the time? Don't you get bored?"

Jemjasee laughed. "Bliss is never boring."

She took deep breaths. Her bare toes scrunched dirt, twigs and rocks. I watched, magnetized by the woman whose strangeness reflected my own, but she was confident, as if only good could come her way.

I turned back to where I first saw her. "How come I can't see your ship?"

"It reflects the terrain it enters. Would you like a tour before I leave?"

The thought of her leaving made me despair. "Later."

She gazed at the vista.

"Dual used to be a popular vacation spot for aliens. They came from different universes, took home souvenirs, gems, cocoa." She glanced at me. "Now, few come. It's hard to enter this dimension with the mounting density of fear. If we fail to navigate through it, we crash."

We watched a flock of birds head south, and I thought about how animals and plants taught me patience and integrity. They weren't afraid of me.

"Can Seren help us?"

"We don't interfere with other civilizations."

We headed toward the cliffs.

"Your mother set up her easel, right there, when Father crossed her path. Over the campfire at Little Harbor, they fell in love."

I imagined my mother, how she must have been then. Her passions great, so consuming they robbed her peace of mind.

"Let's head back. I have work to do, and I must leave soon."

"You just got here," I argued. "What kind of work?"

"I people young planets. Like Paxos, a twin of Dual."

People planets? Earth has a twin? "How do you do that?"

"It can take a day or years to establish a contact. The decision to leave home is always their own."

"Where do the people come from?"

"Many came from here. Now I recruit from other universes. Intergalaticals with humanoid DNA, who through countless incarnations learned and apply the nature of peace." She reached for my hand. "I must go."

"Are you intergalatical?"

"No. Both Father and my mother were Serenians. We share the same forefathers as all humanoids, but without the V-gene."

The mention of my father demanded an answer to my question, and I wouldn't let her go. "What was Father like?"

"He was an artist, like your mother. He designed Seren's Mothership and was known as a great navigator." Tenderness gleamed from her being. "He loved you and your mother."

She put her arm around me, and my sadness seeped away.

"How far away is Paxos?" I said without moving.

"Seven-hundred-thousand light years. In my neighborhood, close-by to Seren."

"With people like me? Mixed?"

"Yes."

I couldn't fathom the distance, nor could I grasp that Earth had a twin where everyone lived in peace. "Can that happen here?"

"If everyone is like-minded."

It didn't seem possible.

Jemjasee walked on as I lingered behind.

"I won't see you again, will I?"

She turned with tears in her eyes.

Why risk her life to come back here? I felt the sting of defeat, a personal failure for myself and my planet. I continued on, missing her before she was gone.

Without command, a ramp and arch appeared.

"How did it do that?"

"The vessel's malleable, chipped to my thoughts."

We went through the dome.

When I walked into the chamber, I thought I was still outside. The structure was invisible, but there was a panel—about twenty feet long with keyboards and buttons, switches, knobs and screens inlaid like mosaics into a control board. The floor too was clear, which gave me the spooky sensation of hovering inches above the ground. A spiral escalator several feet away appeared suspended.

"How tall is it? How wide?"

"It can be limited to design. I prefer space."

In an instant, the ship had an hourglass structure, three tiers and large enough to hold twenty people. "It's more like a rocket than a spaceship."

"That depends."

I stood in the ship turned on its side.

She touched a switch on the console, and a multidimensional planet appeared.

"Paxos," Jemjasee said.

She brought the planet to me. Dwarfed by pillars of granite rock, the smell of pine filtered through a canopy of trees where I glimpsed a purple and orange sunset.

"It looks like Yosemite," I said gazing at several waterfalls.

She placed me in a city where every brightly colored building was oblong or round. Atop a hill, an arrow of lighting flashed by, "The transit system," Jemjasee said. She swooped in close. I stood beside people who looked like me, some different, all humanoids.

Then I found myself on a dirt road beside farmlands and fields of wildflowers. A young man came running over. His attire: a kilt or a skirt with patterns of exotic animals that moved as he ran, his skin a marble wash of lavender and green.

"Hi, I'm Deke." He took in my jeans and denim jacket. "You from Dual?"

"Yes. My name's Gwendolyn. Where are you from, originally?"

"Jura."

"How long have you been here?"

"Four years."

"Do like it?"

"Sure, don't you?" he asked.

"I'm just visiting."

"Oh." He sounded disheartened.

"What kind of animals are here?" I asked.

"Like those on Dual. But they're all vegan, like we are. Everyone has a garden on Paxos. Many, like me are farmers. I grow food for all the animals."

"Vegan lions and wolves?"

He nodded. "We have a common goal, that every breath increases our chances to detach from the V-Gene."

I wanted to touch him to see if his skin was cool or warm like his eyes. "Do you have a family?"

"No, but I want one."

"Me too."

I was back inside the ship, wishing I could have stayed and talked to Deke.

"Peace everywhere?" I asked. "Even the animals?"

"If someone's actions cause harm," Jemjasee said. "They're taken off-planet. Everything, thought or deed, is for the greatest good of all."

I thought about Deke, his skin a watercolor of heavens, reminding me of my mother's paintings.

"Am I eligible?"

"You are."

"And I'd see you, often?"

"Of course."

Could I leave—The Self-Realization Center, Carlos, Maria and the kids?

I went to the arch and looked out at the cliffs. I'd be leaving mom's artwork behind and the emerald ring and earrings she gave me for my sixteenth birthday. Would she be hurt if I took nothing but her memory?

A wistful feeling of all that had been swept over me.

I took a step forward. The ramp rolled onto the ground. I took off my shoes. Sprigs and rocks scuffed my heels. A breeze fluttered strands of hair across my face. I'd be accepted on Paxos. I never considered a husband or child, but now?

I saw Carlos's truck. His tires spewed billows of dust as he headed toward the overlook.

I gazed across the field to my camera and backpack.

Fear had destroyed Mom's life. I mustn't let that happen to me. Perhaps that would be her tribute.

Go Gwendolyn, my mother whispered on the wind. Go.

~~~
~~~

Lines for Anthony Louis

By John Muro

What hurts most is the living and
the knowing that a furious life
could be so easily extinguished
and ladled into a slot of earth
not much wider than a mail slot
tucked inside a sunken garden
that sheltered us from the haze
of a late-summer sun and where
ears could follow the church bell's
loud chorus between verses of
hushed amens and the trespass
of dry, thin-stemmed leaves
that scuttled past like so many
endings, though our dull hearts
were guided from grief to gladness
by your sons and how comfort
came in the listening to decades
strewn with one-too-many wounds
and (how could it be otherwise?)
fewer healings and that youth
fled so quickly from your life

and knowing too, that, despite
our differences, we were so very
much alike and now knowing
that your memory alone lives
on and how the service ended
with the salve of a small bird
flitting between windows wide
with light, having chosen that
particular moment to sing, unbidden,
past sorrow and all that had been
broken and worked its way to joy.


~~~
~~~

In Fragments

By Jonathan Chibuike Ukah

When the sky switches to red
or the sun wears a light jacket,
I will come to you for a cuddle;

Like the dry orange fruits
shedding their old, withered weight,
I am slim and slightly unsteady;

My head is full of glass
with the dreadful pelting of the winds,
my feet wobble in the dimness;

Tears form tinted glasses,
like the tangled, brown screen
of a cobweb on the bark of a tree.

Blundering in my dreams, I stutter
in a pocketful of steamy blood,
the cold sun on my lips.

Now I come to you
lifting the seas into my heart
and letting them flow towards you.

Perhaps you could see me
naked like gazelles on the street,
pacing in the night sky.

I know that somewhere in your heart,
where love has slept off for a while,
you will resurrect me.

You will grant me the ground
on which to rest and grow,
on which to stroll through eternity.


~~~
~~~

Crowned

By Daniel Lockeridge

Could I adjust my words like wings, till they melded
with boughs and bows in which you would be interested?

Could I sing as though dropping from your hug like earth,
or at least speak my poems with the thinnest fire of hurt?

Pull back the burnt leaf of my kiss. You'll spot a gyrfalcon
that has never been seen, in its flames of snow.

You never knew, did you? I was a bright bird, too,
swaying on promise and hunting volcanoes.

Do I write anymore, or plummet… with feather or summers?
Do I know you outside of this mountain range kingdom of flutter

which has risen since I've fallen, through the words' origin—
that place where wings are repositioned upon the magma-whim?

Keep ruling. I'll keep writing like a gyration in ash,
till night is formed like a wing on a crown on the eyelash.

~~~
~~~

After the Ride

By Diana Kurniawan

(For "Fast Car" by Tracy Chapman)

She says she will be married
He just needs to get things straighten out
Maybe get a ring and move out of
The shelter and just camp outside

Walking did nothing good but her
Shoes still works after all those miles
By the freeway entrance to the railroad tracks
From the city courts to the church dining hall

No one even looks at her with all
The play money currency in bottle caps
He just needs to lay off his hands from her
Neck clenching under the bridge raping her

The skin on her hands cracked
From the cold winters and no gloves nor blankets
The lips are not only for begging or selling
She says he loves her even without her body

She is now making her veil with aluminum foil
Twisted to a loop with a long layer of white napkin
He just needs the priest to give the ceremony
She thinks the park is a good and proper place

It's now too late for babies or mending her heart
She says she'll work with what she's got
It is not everyday a woman gets her man
Don't matter if he's got tough hands or not


~~~
~~~

It Started to Rain

By Laura S. Martineé

The light went out. It escaped from that peak moment of shared silences. It began to rain again. I listened as my thoughts were disorganized to the rhythm of a warm strangeness poured over a dark forest of orphan words of syllables. Incessant confusion. A mixture of environments shaded by entities that I barely recognize. And the space that remains between what once was and what only happened in the corner of the blue tale is compromised by the strong absence of hope.

More than a thousand things happened; new people arriving, familiar faces dissipating between the colorful horizon and the imposing sun. However, the constant feeling of dispossession and disorientation does not give any respite.

The wait is prolonged. Continue waiting as a guideline to follow...perhaps to the longed for or perhaps the unexpected.

~~~
~~~

Accordia

By Gary Beck

I kept a confident, positive look on my face as the Governor of Louisiana, Alicia deVray, prepared to sign the document that would enact the first free drug community in the world. She turned and looked at me, I nodded encouragingly, she looked at the horde of reporters holding cameras, phones, recording devices and signed. There was a long moment of silence, then a round of weak, tentative applause from the legislators. Alicia wasn't looking her usual ebullient self as she chatted with legislators, supporters and opponents of the controversial free drug community. CNN asked me to say a few words and I praised the Governor and the state legislators for their forward thinking in pioneering a solution to end the criminal distribution of drugs. Fox News accused me of destroying the fabric of America by giving away free drugs. I smiled politely and said:

"We will end drug crime in America," then I followed Alicia to her office.

As soon as we were alone, she murmured:

"This better work, M, or they'll lynch us on the biggest tree in Baton Rouge."

"Don't worry, Al. You'll dangle a lot prettier than me," which made her giggle.

The day we met at first year Tulane Law, she said: 'Call me Al'. I replied: 'Call me M', and our friendship was born. We became best friends through school, stayed close as her career soared in the

Orleans Parish District Attorney's office, elected D.A, the State Senate, now in her second term as Governor of the Pelican State. Despite our entirely different directions, mine starting in the Orleans Parish Public Defender's office that led to our occasional clash in the courtroom which she invariably won, since most of my clients were obviously guilty to judge and jury alike. But as Al climbed the political ladder, I started a foundation using my trust fund until I could raise money whose express purpose was to legalize drugs so we could end the criminal drug trade that was polluting and corrupting America.

Once Al got to the State Senate we didn't spend as much time together, but we texted, phoned and skyped regularly. When I came up with the idea of a planned community where drugs were free she teased me unmercifully. Her attitude began to change when a benefactor donated five million dollars and promised more. I immediately hired a Nobel prize-winning economist, a criminal psychologist, a statistical analyst and a software developer. We started by reviewing the bulk of the literature on drugs and crime, which was extensive. My particular focus was on criminal profits, drug cartels and the cost to the nation for drug-related arrests, trials and incarceration. When the cost to society passed one hundred billion dollars a year I started thinking about solutions.

Al laughed at me when I first proposed a community where drugs were free and everything else resembled a normal community. There would be a police department, fire, sanitation, EMT, courthouses, stores, shops, restaurants, three levels of housing dependent on employment and income, or subsidy. For those who didn't want to work but wanted to use drugs there was basic housing, food allotment, health services and a monthly stipend. Al stopped laughing when I showed her the cost of operating a free drug community of 5,000 population was between 70 and 75% less than a regular community with drug crime.

"What do you want from me, M?"

"If I can't get another state to let us start a demonstration project, let me do it here."

"You know how controversial this would be. It would start a firestorm of righteous objections."

"Sure. But we know that prohibition never works. The 18th Amendment, Volstead Act, banned booze, then gave birth to organized crime. The drug trade is international, poisoning our country and much of the world."

"Why couldn't you commit to saving the environment?"

"Because I didn't want to spend my life fighting the fossil fuel industry."

When we finished our first demonstration model, I asked my benefactor for ten million dollars to fund the construction and staffing of the community, with the goal of it becoming economically self-sufficient. He promised the money and I began searching for the right state to start our project.

I didn't try Nevada because the gambling industry was a negative element in the American way of life. The Governor of New York was publicly outraged, but wished me luck privately. The Governor of California thought I meant a drug-free community and offered help, until an aide whispered in his ear what I intended. I got a very polite farewell. The Governor of Florida kept asking where I'd get my drugs and derided my explanation that we'd buy them on the international market.

"You'll be supporting the drug business," he insisted.

"That's a byproduct, sir. We'll demonstrate that when drugs are legal the related crime and corruption will disappear."

"It sounds like a hippie idea. Not interested."

Arizona, Massachusetts, Indiana and North Carolina wouldn't even give me a hearing. Which led me back to my pal Al, in Louisiana.

I found a struggling town upstate on the bank of the Quachita River that with an infusion of capital would be a great location. I visited the mayor and gave him an overview of the project, then operational details. His biggest concern was with the extreme addicts and the possible threats to the townspeople.

"The neighborhood of new housing will be separated from the rest of the town, with most of what they'll need right there. People will be selected so we'll know they are basically content with their allotments. If they want better houses, they'll have to work for it. Your police department will be supported by a highly-trained, ex-military group who will patrol 24/7 and peacefully resolve any problems. We'll install a sophisticated camera and monitoring system to support law enforcement. The money we'll bring in for construction, services and operations will bring your town back to life."

"We have 1,800 citizens who would have to approve any project."

"If you and your main supporters approve our project, we'll only need a good size majority, say 1,400 to 1,500."

He grinned. "You make a good case. I'll arrange for you to meet with some concerned citizens. If they approve you can present it to everyone at a town hall meeting."

"I'll bring my experts."

One evening two weeks later we met with the town council and prominent citizens. They were dazzled by my Nobel Prize winning economist, fascinated by my criminal psychologist and impressed by my director of security, a former Ranger Lieutenant-Colonel and a childhood friend, Paul Morein. A few citizens were afraid of being known as a drug town, but the promise of the infusion of lots of money won them over. Only the sheriff was resistant. I won him over with a single statement.

"The supplemental security force will cooperate fully with your department and provide new cars and equipment."

He looked at me suspiciously. "Do you hunt?"

"Not any more, sheriff."

"Do you fish?"

"Not for a while."

"Are you related to Jean Dubonne?"

"He was my grandfather. Did you know him?"

"I met him a few times when he was Attorney General. A good man."

"A very good man," I asserted.

He gave me a big grin. "I'll support your project, son."

I smiled back. "Thanks, sheriff. That'll make things a lot easier."

The town hall meeting a few weeks later was a study in local politics. Everyone important spoke out in favor of the project and almost all the citizens approved. The usual opposition of conservatives wanting things as they were, a few evangelicals and some scaredy cats objected vigorously, but to no avail. After an intense, short campaign the vote was 1,726 against 53, with 21 abstaining. So with the town's approval and with the Governor's signature, we were ready to establish a legal free drug community.

Now that the town committed to the project, I sent them summary copies of the contract that each applicant would have to sign to participate. I had drawn up a complex document that would protect the town and the project sponsors from legal repercussions, which included a short series of rules:

1) Abstain from all criminal acts.

2) Do not operate vehicles, machinery, or any dangerous equipment while under the influence of intoxicants.

3) Possession of weapons is forbidden.

4) Abide by the laws of the community.

5) No resuscitation from overdoses.

There were more rules but there was time to refine them as we started the recruiting process for approximately 3,000 candidates for the program. The next goal would be to finalize the planning of the community with housing, stores, restaurants, a drug dispensing building, security building, social services... The list went on. Everything was outlined in the project proposal. Now we would have to construct the new town while we selected the population.

We had decided on initial recruitment efforts in New Orleans, Baton Rouge, Shreveport, Metairie and Lafayette, assuming word would spread to the Parishes. Of course if we didn't get enough free drug wanters from Louisiana, we'd expand the search to neighboring states. I was walking on air. Years of hope and effort were about to become a reality.

The next step of implementing the plan was to acquire the land which was easy with the cooperation of the town authorities. They wanted to remove one holdout with eminent domain, which I rejected. I went to see the crusty old farmer and told him his new neighbors would be busy, but wouldn't impose a threat to him. When I told him I was happy with his remaining there and opposed eminent domain he became friendly and invited me to go fishing with him. It was obvious we didn't have to complete all the new living facilities at once, but we had to have all support services ready when the first... I had to find a name for them... Accords. I'll try that.

I went over the list of the services that had to come first and a supermarket and medical services were still the priority. We had been negotiating with several supermarket chains who were interested in opening in... Accordia?... Now we'd finalize our choice. They would be guaranteed a minimum of two years of earnings by the Accordia foundation. We'd have time to work out the economics of the community so people could start paying for their purchases. It was easy to get nurses who were well paid and delighted to work in a new well supplied, well equipped facility. We made our arrangement to hire medical school graduates as interns, who would work under the supervision of two local doctors.

I was going to throw a party and invite all my friends, the project planners and of course my favorite Governor, Al. After all the project was officially launched. It could take a year or more to see the proof of the theory that free drugs did away with related crime. So, it was time to celebrate the beginning of the dream scheme come true.


~~~
~~~

If the Body Is a Temple of the Holy Spirit, Then What Is the Mind?

By Jonathan Fletcher

Where my church
doesn't understand,
I think you might.
I pray you would.

More than saving,
I need an ear.
More than miracles,
I need an advocate.

Like you,
I've been accused
of being possessed.
Like you,
I've frightened others.

Though no demon
lurks within,
I often fear myself,
I often fear my moods.

Maybe you feared yours,
as well—when extreme,
able to heal the sick,
when extreme,
able to cleanse the Temple.


~~~
~~~

1790*

By M F Drummy

For some reason I feel like
Emily Dickinson today –
A timid, untitled
Bird – wings clipped –

Descending, Zen-like,
Through nesting dolls
Of Loneliness toward
The unwelcome potsherds

Of Deceit – fearsome relics
Of the archaeology of
The Soul – a Life in chaos,
Nature unbound from

Intention – random, drifting –
Daffodils wrapped in Wax –
Will I never get my Ducks
in a row again?

~~~
~~~

* While there are enough disagreements to fill a small library concerning the number of untitled poems Emily Dickinson actually composed, the first Harvard University Press paperback edition of The Poems of Emily Dickinson, edited by R. W. Franklin and published in 2005, tallies 1789.*

I Beg for Scraps for Breakfast

By Elizabeth Adan

there's something like the act of foraging
or wearing tan in the forest and snacking on ruby lobster
            mushrooms

we learned to scrape bark from trees and sell it
the moss in the soft places where we left soft steps
and I got turned around and made a break running toward the car

the foxgloves were as high as my shoulders
and the flowers left pollen in the tips of my hair
the orange of chanterelle cousins and filling the backpack my dog
            carried proudly

how wise we stars are who drive over bridges
and know how to knock and make the music
the swamps and the trails and running in morning
the mist never cracks but the mushrooms keep growing

I knew brown like your boots after wading in the river
like the brown of the night sky or the dark stars or the ones who
            give life
extra roll logs sausage hills

the competition
the old of it all as shotgun blast hills expose fire red weeds

I fill your backpack with arrogant handfuls
the fire grows larger until I'm uncomfortable
your rattan baskets
too much risk for too little reward

I guess I knew the tan of the bags would fade when we hung them
        from tree branches

more time for the ironed flat picnic blankets
more time for the wicker
can you crawl
cage antique with tongues of silver
like crab
the pride of the rest of your life
we crawl
toward the sunlight in the morning exiting the flappy wet tent
toward the beach from the river when frigid water regret reaches
        your bones

those glamorous words
those dogs and the splinters in the wood slats

wrapped in towels all cold wet and cowering
sleeping in the trunk of the car with the windows open to let the
        mosquitoes in
we were just glitter flight kites and road wrap succulent gardeners

we crash like china in rusty wooden cabinets
and the crinkle of tin foil freshly shaped for your head
vanilla sweet kettle melt
hats on pedestals and holding you up toward the moon

the pride of the forest waking each morning to kiss the skyline
gape in awe at the clouds sprinting across the sky
her wide lips reach for us and you say yes first
mist never clearing

later
in the clearing
the fireweed blooms and the foxgloves tell me to go home
ruby lobster and time worn blended families
no sleep for the wicked and no rust for the woke
the night opens big plans deep like demon deals

everything
all open and so woven
straw kingdom soldiers and the backs the bones of arguments

and then yes
we say yes
to the issues in the wind floating with a dandelion seed
and I am a vector of hope
a conductive ray of sunlight radiation
a bride vacation

we're tan for the taking
with a horse saddle and a brand new silver barn
we're peeled open on purpose

we stand with hips touching shoulders and hands full of marigolds
the baskets are broken and dripping all over the floor
the water filled with fish

I beg for scraps for breakfast
the avocado toasts

in pink pajamas by the oil fire grease explosion
the flowers wilt in the heat

outside
the sounds of the bells grow louder
cawing crows change the whole mood of the wind

so angry
the desperate crack of branches as squirrels chase my dogs

what yellow world hope is this tan warm sunset trying to tell me
we see the flow move and the mixture melt and then you find out
          you're allergic
spend a wish on the idea of that first connection

there used to be our bountied wings painted on the side of the
          parking garage
and alley hookah art murals that evolved by the month and grew
          thick with texture

you grew two heads
one for loving and one for life
smoke clouds circle around them both

reach back to hold your own angel hands
an embassy of eagles
the belts tighten

glowing computer cooked robot warrior, all egg cracked

looks depressed

an aura of tan and embarrassment

nothing left


~~~
~~~

Watercolor

By Nick Young

From her earliest memories, Laura Bishop had been entranced by summer flowers. Every year, behind the small clapboard farmhouse where she lived with her mother and father, the hillside that sloped gently up to a stand of thick woods became a dazzling carpet— coneflower and corn poppy, blue flax, Indian blanket, goldenrod and New England aster. These were the names taught to her by her mother.

"Now, your aunt Elizabeth, a very smart woman, indeed," her mother had said, "knows every one of those flowers by their Latin names. She learned them at the college in Carbondale. I just know them by what we call them here. Good enough for me. In that, I am in agreement with your father. Why do we need a foreign name when we have a perfectly fine one in good, old American?"

But the little girl had not the slightest grasp of the fuss about what to call the flowers. She only knew that she reveled in their palette of yellows and scarlets, purples and blues splashed amidst the lush grasses as she ran with exultation to the shade of a broad willow at the crest of the hill. Sometimes her beloved collie Miss Doxie would run with her, bounding up the slope, barking excitedly and dashing in circles under the willow waiting for Laura to catch up. And while she very much liked the companionship of her dog, what filled her young heart even more was going alone, especially on July afternoons when a hot wind rushed up from the south to stir the flowers to murmuring.

When she was thirteen, Laura was given a set of watercolor paints for her birthday—a rectangular tin case with a hinged lid containing a dozen squares of paint along with a small wooden-handled brush that fit inside and a spiral notebook of special art paper.

"Now you can paint your flowers and have them with you all the year round," her mother had said.

And so it was. Each day when the hillside was in bloom, Laura would venture forth, sometimes dutifully accompanied by Miss Doxie, at other times by herself, with her painting gear inside a coarse-woven burlap satchel that hung from a strap over her shoulder. On the hottest days, she favored the shade of the willow tree; when the weather was milder, she would find a spot in the middle of the glorious flowers themselves.

At first the paintings were crude as she struggled with the trickiness of using the brush and getting the mix of water and paint right; but as time passed, with diligent practice, she became more sure of herself and it showed in her work. And as her confidence grew, she began to venture farther from home, through the timber at the top of the slope and out into a meadow more remote. It, too, was resplendent with wildflowers, and it gladdened her spirit to make a place for herself amid the blooms and paint to her heart's content. She also made time for reverie, setting her brush aside and lying back, closing her eyes and imagining she was transported far away to exotic places on a magic floral carpet.

It was especially warm the summer of 1960, the summer Laura Bishop turned fifteen. It was a time of struggle in her life. School had been difficult, particularly her geometry class. The concepts were hard to grasp and her resistance to learning them festered into resentment over having to take the course at all when she only wanted to study literature and art.

But it was more than schoolwork. There were the swirling teenage social pressures to deal with in her small school. She was not one of the popular girls. She was too plain-looking, bookish in round tortoise shell glasses, her hair cut page-boy style. Out of insecurity, she smiled infrequently and spoke quietly. That did not attract the attention of boys. They were invariably drawn to the cuter, more outgoing girls.

And all the while there was what was gathering inside her, building like a May thunderstorm. She was in the midst of her transformation into womanhood. Her slender body bore the more outward signs; and within, new feelings were stirring, stealing upon her as the ivory moon hung outside the window of her room while she lay between the sheets of her bed, impulses that were both exciting and frightening. At first, she did not know how to respond except to push them away. She felt too embarrassed to approach her mother— what would she say? She had no close girlfriend she could confide in. But once, in the bathroom at church, she had overheard two older girls giggling and whispering. Though what they said shocked her at first, she did not forget. And before long, when she turned out the light beside her bed and night's shadows and a rising inner heat enveloped her, she began to discover herself in a new way.

Laura's one constant through the turmoil and frustration was her artwork. She had continued to paint and had taken a class in art appreciation. Before school let out, she signed up for a summer painting program organized by her art teacher, Mr. Bellinghausen. At the first meeting in mid-June, there were only six other students, three girls and two boys from her school and a girl who was new to her and the others. She introduced herself as Colleen—"Everybody calls me Coll"—Wilkins. She said she was seventeen, her parents were divorced and she had just moved from St. Louis with her mother. She was interested in all kinds of drawing and painting, she said, especially watercolor.

That immediately got Laura's attention, so after Mr. Bellinghausen dismissed the group with the assignment to return the following week with a drawing or painting of a natural setting, Laura overcame her shyness and introduced herself to the new girl.

Coll was taller than Laura by an inch or two, with the lithe body of a dancer. She had long blonde hair tied in a ponytail and very lively blue eyes that flashed as often as her easy smile.

"What do you like to paint?" Laura asked.

"Just about anything, really. I'm not much good at portrait-type stuff, but I like still life, nature scenes..."

"How about wildflowers?"

"Oh, yes," Coll answered with enthusiasm. "I used to go to a park in St. Louis that was close to our apartment. It was loaded with all kinds of flowers, and I'd draw and paint there. Too bad we don't have any where our house is now." Laura, whose normal reserve normally held her back with someone new, felt it slip away with this girl.

"Well, I live on a farm," she said, "and we've got all the flowers you could want—acres, it seems. Do you think your mom would let you come out and paint them with me?" Coll brightened.

"I'm sure she wouldn't mind. She'll be happy I made a new friend."

Two days later, after an exchange of phone calls between the mothers, Coll drove out to the farm. Mrs. Bishop fixed a lunch of sandwiches and lemonade, talking cheerfully all the while. The girls were polite but restrained in front of the older woman. It wasn't until they took up their paints and headed out the back door that they began to relax, become more animated and talk more freely.

Coll was immediately struck by the wild beauty of the flower-covered slope.

"There are so many, and they're so *beautiful,*" she marveled as she walked side-by-side with Laura. Miss Doxie barked and scampered up ahead to the shade of the willow tree.

Thus began the bond between the two girls, which grew as they spent more time together, painting and trying to make sense of their adolescent lives. Despite growing up in such different places, they found quite a lot in common. Both were frustrated with school, disliking most of what they had to learn. They were convinced adults didn't understand them. Neither of them had much good to say about boys. Because of her shyness and complete lack of experience, they were largely baffling to Laura. Not so with Coll. She found boys coarse and repulsive.

"They're not like us. They only think with one thing," she said, with a slight shudder, "and it isn't this," she finished, pointing to her head.

As the summer spooled out, the girls were with each other more often than not, sometimes spending most of the day away from the farm with a picnic lunch Laura's mother packed for them. And they became more familiar with each other, relaxed and uninhibited. This was Coll's nature, and it helped Laura emerge from her shell.

When they were apart, Coll remained very much on Laura's mind, a companion as she wandered the meadows by day and by her side late into the night. She was experiencing a kind of exhilaration, a freedom of spirit she had never known.

One day, after Coll had returned home, Laura found that she had left the bag with her painting supplies behind. Laura decided to take it to her room for safekeeping. When she lifted it onto the shelf in her closet, a piece of notebook paper slipped out onto the floor. Laura retrieved it and saw that there were lines of what looked like poetry written on it in blue ballpoint. She recognized Coll's handwriting.

"...my tongue is broken;
a thin flame runs under
my skin; seeing nothing,

hearing only my own ears
drumming, I drip with sweat;
trembling shakes my body

What Laura read sent a tremor through her. Were these Coll's words? Laura replaced the paper in her friend's bag and tucked it into the closet.

But she could not put the verse out of her mind. It deepened what she already felt, that being close to Coll was not like having a sister. It stirred Laura in a different way, a way that was quite unsororal.

The afternoon of August 18 was deep in the midst of the southern Illinois dog days. With school starting up in another week, Laura and Coll were intent on spending as much of their remaining free time together as they could, so they planned for a long excursion, eating an early lunch at the farm before setting off. On this trip, Miss Doxie was left behind at the house where she could doze on the shaded porch.

High overhead, the midday sun was fierce, so the girls, each wearing wide straw hats, made their way quickly up the slope to the relative coolness of the sprawling willow. There they sat close together fanning themselves, talking and giggling. After a time, Laura reached for her satchel of paints.

"Wait," said Coll, taking hold of the other girl's arm, "I've got an idea. Let's take our things and go to the other meadow."

"But, Coll, it's *so hot*," Laura protested.

"We won't stay long, just a while," Coll answered. "I love that it's so far from everything—and everybody. It's *ours*, our *secret*, just the two of us." Laura could see an intensity in the other girl's face and it triggered an unexpected thrill in her.

"Alright," she answered. "Just the two of us." They gathered their things and left the shade of the willow, walking a distance through a thick stand of old trees, mostly oak and cottonwoods, before cutting across a shallow gully, up a long incline and over to a secluded half-acre swath of meadow that bordered the bank of a tiny stream. Coll reached out and took Laura's hand and, giving it a gentle squeeze, led her down and through the flowers to a grassy patch near the lip of the rill.

"Right here," said Coll. "Let's paint right here."

"There's not much shade," Laura replied, glancing around. Sun dappled the ground as light sifted through the arching branches of a tall oak.

"Enough," Coll said. "Besides, the sun feels *so good* today." She was usually quick to complain when the weather was especially oppressive. But even though Laura found Coll's reaction to the heat odd, she would acquiesce. As the weeks had passed and the two of them had grown closer, Laura had come to be in thrall to the older girl. For her it seemed only natural. Her friend was opening her, drawing her out of herself, helping her see the world in new ways.

They unpacked their paints and water, brushes and paper. There was also a quart canning jar of lemonade Laura's mother had prepared. It was still fairly cold, so Laura unscrewed the lid and they passed the jar between them, laughing as they drank.

"I think it's time to paint," Laura said at last. So, they took up their brushes, wet them and began mixing colors. Laura turned her attention to the trees and stream, while Coll returned as she did on each of their outings to the beauty of the flowers. The girls had painted quietly for a quarter-hour or so when Coll paused.

"You know what I want us to do?" She looked devilishly at her companion.

"What?"

"I want us to get a *real* tan."

"What are you talking about?"

"Here, I'll show you," Coll said, never taking her eyes from Laura as she unbuttoned her white cotton blouse—

"Coll!"

—reached behind her back, unsnapped her bra and slid out of it.

"What are you *doing?*" Laura said, eyes wide, flustered at her friend's unexpected act and her nakedness.

"Now you," Coll commanded.

"I will *not*," Laura answered, her face flushing.

"You trust me, don't you?"

"Well, yes, but…"

"Well, then, come on," Coll continued. "Here, let me help." And before Laura could protest further, Coll reached out and began undoing the buttons on her friend's blouse. When she finished, she drew the blouse open.

"Now, you finish."

"But, *Coll*…" Laura tried to object, but her resolve was weakening as there arose within her a sensation she could not deny. Her eyes flashed around as if she was worried she was being watched.

"Go ahead," Coll said, "there's nobody else, just you and me."

"Well…," Laura began tentatively, using her right hand to undo the clasp of her brassiere and remove it.

"Now," said Coll, "lay down by me." With a self-conscious giggle, Laura joined her friend in putting aside their straw hats and lying side by side, squeezing their eyes tightly against the glare. After a long moment, Coll breathed a deep sigh. "Mmmm, it feels *so good*. Doesn't it feel wonderful?"

"Yes," Laura answered softly, titillated by Coll's proximity and the heat pulsing against her pale torso.

"I've got another idea," Coll said, rolling onto her side to face Laura. The younger girl raised a hand to shield her eyes and looked at her friend.

"What?" Coll searched Laura's face.

"I want you to just lay there with your eyes closed."

"Okay. Then what?"

"Nothing. Just lay there—and promise not to open your eyes."

"And what are you going to do?" Coll, again with a hint of devilment in her smile, answered,

"That's a secret."

"Coll, come on."

"You trust me, right? You said you trusted me."

"I do."

"Okay, then, lay back down and close your eyes." Laura complied, while Coll got to her feet and removed her blouse. "No peeking, promise?"

"Promise."

Laura heard Coll move away, but she kept to her word not to look. *What was she up to?* Laura lightly brushed a hand across her skin which, despite the heat, sent a deep shiver through her. The world was far away. The only sounds were the gentle murmuring of the brook and the rising and falling thrum of cicadas in the trees. *Where could she have gone?*

Presently, Laura heard the footsteps of her friend returning.

"Where have you been, girl?" Coll laughed.

"A surprise, remember? Now, no peeking, please." With that, Coll knelt next to Laura and, from the large bunch of wildflowers she clutched to her chest, began strewing the blossoms onto Laura's bare torso—coneflower and corn poppy, blue flax, Indian blanket, goldenrod and New England aster. As the flowers began covering her, Laura picked up their scent and her breath caught.

"Coll..."

When she had dropped the last of the flowers, Coll bent close to Laura's ear and whispered,

"A thin flame runs under my skin." For Laura, that moment finally unlocked a door that, though not always conscious of it, she had been pressing against harder each time she was with Coll or when the image of the older girl stole upon her late at night. Without opening her eyes, Laura's arms encircled Coll and drew her close.

Overhead, the August sun shimmered down. The girls' legs entwined, knocking over the water jar, spilling the liquid across their paintings, causing the colors to bleed one into the other.

~~~

Watercolor first appeared in Backchannels Journal
~~~

Smoke and Mirrors

By John RC Potter

The images are now almost reflected
and through smoke, truth is deflected.
In my mind are reflections of the past
and are found in the one I loved last.
How is it we can bear so much pain
and yet learn to love all over again?
The pain of loss encompasses our souls
and then threatens to consume us whole.
Unrequited love perhaps lives the longest
and the one giving up can be the strongest.
Seasons change but it seems people don't
and although they could they just won't.
Through the smoke appears your face
and your mirror tilts but hangs in place.

I would like to extinguish the fire
or at least stop the smoke from rising;
I want to walk up to this internal mirror
and see your reflection looking back at me.

If I could, I would pull the truth from you,
one tenuous strand at a time;
to breathe life through that mask you wear
until the heat of my love melts it away.

Failing all this I must give up, turn away, leave
and hope you make it through the smoke alone;
never to see what happens when, or if, or how
you face the mirror of your making.

Smoke and mirrors, mirrors, and smoke:
one obscures the truth, the other deflects it.
I will endure the fire until there's no more smoke:
To pick up the pieces when the mirror breaks.


~~~
~~~

Release Recurring

By Rikki Santer

(after Céline Sciamma's *Portrait of a Lady on Fire*)

Amniotic churning of rough sea, the painter reinvents herself.
Scaling pelvic bone of cliff, instinct will harness her hunger
to be twinned. In an 18th century chateau immense quiet is
alert to isolate each rustle of petticoat, shivering tongues of
candle or fireplace, scratches from charcoal on tight canvases
of uncalcined umber. Eyes of the painter and her muse agree
in the craft of craving capture, rapture of their mouths sends
paper lanterns to the moon, pubis cradles self-portrait, perfect
skin luminous, beholder becomes beheld, beheld becomes
beholder. Legend maroons them on this remote shore
where time and timelessness intersect. Their gazes for each
other fixed in tableaus. Color bars of Vivaldi, what another
Orpheus chooses, wedding dress apparition portends.
A woman's world takes charge—a cappella canticle with
witchy bonfire, hem catches flame. With cedar root,
pennyroyal and skewer, a young housekeeper brings down
the flowers of pregnancy and painter takes her place
as rare recorder. Art always seeks its fulcrum between
liberation and captivity. Muse finally released to canvas.

Lovers released from patriarchy to the salve of recurring
recollection deep in their bones.

Muse finally released to canvas because Art always seeks its
fulcrum between liberation and captivity. Young housekeeper
brings down the flowers of pregnancy with cedar root, pennyroyal,
and skewer, while the painter takes her place as rare recorder.
Hem catches flame. A cappella canticle with witchy bonfire.
A woman's world takes charge. Color bars of Vivaldi, what
another Orpheus chooses. Wedding dress apparition portends.
Their gazes for each other fixed in tableaus where time and
timelessness intersect. Legend maroons them on a remote shore.
Beholder becomes beheld, beheld becomes beholder. Perfect skin
luminous, pubis cradles self-portrait. Rapture of their mouths
sends paper lanterns to the moon. Eyes of the painter
and her muse agree in the craft of craving capture. Scratches from
charcoal on tight canvases of umber. shivering tongues of candles
and fireplaces, rustle of petticoats. The immense quiet alert
to isolate in an 18th century chateau. Instinct harnessing
the hunger to be twined, she scaled pelvic bones of cliff.
The painter reinvented herself. Amniotic churning of rough sea.


~~~
~~~

The Devil's Dog

By Sarah Das Gupta

A cold east wind was blowing through the graveyard of Holy Trinity Church at Rainsford that November evening. The old elms were bending before the gale, dark clouds hung low over the fields. The broken crosses on the oldest graves leant at odd angles like bony figures pointing at the bleak countryside.

Inside the vestry, Mark Thompson shivered as he tidied up the papers he had been reading. He was beginning to regret volunteering to look through the drawers of papers and objects which seemed to have been untouched for years. Copies of old parish magazines, going back before the Second World War, lists of graves, receipts for grass cutting, rotas for flower arranging were mixed up with old vestments, a censer, torn hymn books and sermon notes. Just as he was about to close the dark oak cupboard, he noticed a small drawer at the very back. Leaning into the dark interior of the cupboard, Mark pulled out a wadge of papers. The parchment was thin and yellowing at the edges The writing belonged to a much earlier period. From his work at the local museum, Mark guessed the papers dated from the fifteenth or sixteenth centuries.

Sitting in a shabby leather chair, he started reading the old script. The light in the vestry was dim, the prehistoric oil fire, inadequate. Yet the story told in the manuscript was so disturbing, that Mark ignored the chill in the room and the flickering shadows around him. He began to make notes as he read the faded script.

'It had been St Lucy's Day, 1597, the shortest day of the year, the bleak Winter Solstice. The elite of the Sunday congregation sat in the box pews. The Squire and his family in front. The farm workers and servants crowded at the back. It was just as the vicar climbed into the pulpit that it happened. A gale was raging outside the church, lightning lit up the stained-glass windows depicting hideous devils torturing dead sinners with pitchforks and daggers. The heavy oak doors crashed open, as if the entrance to Hell had appeared. A huge black hound, its eyes like burning saucers, leapt onto two petrified peasants, snapping their necks like matchsticks. Then closer to the altar, this devilish brute shrivelled up a hapless man "like a piece of leather scorched in a hot fire."

'Howling fiendishly, the monster of a hound moved on to the next village, leaving scorch marks, the devil's own fingerprints, on the church doors.'

At the end of the account, Mark read: 'All down the church in midst of fire/ the hellish monster flew/ and passing onward to the quire/ he many people slew.'

Just as he reached this point, the light went out. The room was pitch dark, except for the red glow of the paraffin fire. Gathering the papers together, Mark turned down the wick of the fire and locked the vestry door.

He hurried through the churchyard, a strange red glow hanging over the graves under the dark yews. A bone chilling howl echoed above the sound of the gale as Mark opened the door of his car.

o   o   o

Later that evening, Mark returned to the papers he had found in the vestry cupboard. Near the bottom of the pile the paper and writing noticeably changed. The texture and condition of the manuscript suggested it was from a more recent time. The neat copper writing was typical of the Victorian era and the incident recorded appeared to be based on a local newspaper report. As he started to read, in the distance the town clock tolled midnight. Yet there was something so compelling about these old papers that made him continue.

'The November of 1855 had been unusually cold and stormy along the east coast. The North Sea tides had been high and destructive for most of the Autumn. Near Cromar, the cliffs had crashed into the sea, leaving abandoned houses hanging on the edge of the remaining coastline as the waves pounded the rocks and debris below, like a frenzied monster awaiting feeding time.

'The evening of the 15th the night tide had been higher than usual. Waves washed over the promenade in Skegness. At fishing ports, like Lowestoft and Yarmouth, the life boats had been on alert. At Southwold, a schoolboy had been washed out to sea. In the lighthouse at Rainsford, the Light Keeper and his assistant were probably finishing their dinners, washed down with a light ale. The wind was approaching gale force. Along the coast, life guards watched the waves hitting the lighthouse. The spray was so high that it washed over the top. For a second the whole building disappeared in a watery blur.'

Mark stopped reading. For a moment he saw the scene clearly. The terrifying power of the sea. The two men trapped in the middle of it all. He had been in the lighthouse once and felt seasick with the waves all around and the sense of imprisonment, of claustrophobia in the tiny round sitting room with its scanty furnishings. He turned back to the beautifully written manuscript.

'Suddenly, the coast guards at Rainsford saw something extraordinary which they later testified to on oath. On top of the cliffs, appeared a huge black dog. Even above the wind they heard its chilling howl. Enormous, saucer-shaped eyes burnt and glowed through the gathering darkness. The dog leapt off the cliffs. As if riding on the swirling mist, this heart-stopping beast was carried to the top storey of the lighthouse. At the same moment, an enormous wave broke over the building. The lighthouse disappeared in a wall of foaming water.

'When it re-emerged from the misty spray, the spectral hound had vanished.'

Mark felt a chill in the room. He switched on a second lamp. Instinctively he looked out at the black storm clouds, scudding across the sky as he turned back to the account.

'Next morning apparently the storm had vanished. The sea was as calm as a mill pond, not a white horse in sight. The coast guards dragged a boat down the beach, intending to row out to the lighthouse, now gleaming in the pale winter sunshine. Preparing to push the boat into the sea, they suddenly saw a body on the shoreline being gently lifted and lowered by the incoming tide. They recognised the Light Keeper and pulled the water-logged corpse up the beach. As they turned it over, water dribbled from a horribly savaged mouth and face. The right hand and wrist were missing.

'The local policeman later accompanied them to the lighthouse. They climbed the stairs in some trepidation, their footsteps echoing in the nervous silence. Only the sound of the waves washing over the dark rocks whispered eerily in the background. Fearful they slowly opened the door to the small sitting room. The assistant keeper sat bolt upright in a chair, a look of sheer terror on his face. There was no sign of a struggle. He had literally died of fright.'

Mark heard the clock strike again. It was almost 2 am. Despite the late hour, he lay awake, listening to the wind moaning and the sound of thunder in the distance.

o   o   o

Two years had passed. Mark, busy with a new job in a land surveyor's office and a part-time university course, had not had the time to research the stories of the Black Dog any further. At least he now understood why the local football team were known as 'The Black Dogs'!

One day in late August, Mark's Sunday afternoon reverie in the sunny back garden was unexpectedly disturbed.

'Hey, Mark! Have you read this in the local rag?'

He woke from dozing to see his girlfriend, Steph, waving a copy of the 'Rainsford Echo' in front of him.

'No, I only buy it for the adverts. Remember, we've been looking for an old weather vane for the cottage?'

'Well, you'll be interested in the re-appearance of the infamous Black Dog. You were obsessed with it a couple of years ago!'

Mark sat up quickly. 'Has there been another sighting of him?'

'Well, only his skeleton, thank goodness. I for one, don't want to face mutilated corpses next time I go swimming!'

'Where's the skeleton. How do they know it's Black Dog? If he's the devil's dog, he can't die.'

'Your mum was saying they've been excavating up at Rainsford Castle. Found it buried inside the bailey.'

Mark was already reading the somewhat dramatic headline, 'Black Dog on the Prowl!'

Next minute, he was half-way down the garden, dragging a reluctant Steph behind him.

'We must see this before they fill it in!'

The ruined castle, a popular tourist sight, was just outside the town. The entrance to the inner courtyard had been blocked off but a few curious onlookers were hanging around.

'You see, you can't get in. You've dragged me here for nothing.'

'Can't get in? Just watch me!'

Mark bent down beneath the barrier, ignoring the bored policeman on duty. He went straight to the site where the digging was taking place. Steph followed dubiously behind.

'Hi, I'm Mark Thompson. I'm the guy who found the papers in Trinity Church. Must have been a couple of years ago. I'm still really interested in this whole story. Hope you don't mind us trespassing.'

'That's ok. We're just trying to stop a crowd of sightseers traipsing about.' A grey-haired man wiped his muddy hands down the back of his already clay-stained jeans.

Steph looked curiously round the cobbled yard. She pictured the scene on a misty day, the sound of horses' hoofs on the grey stones, the dogs barking excitedly, elegant ladies leaning from the lead casements. She was brought back to reality by Mark's excited exclamation, 'Look at that skeleton. The beast must have weighed over 90 kilos and measured at least 2 metres, standing on its hindlegs.'

Steph felt a cold chill. She shivered, despite the sunlight, as she gazed down at a remarkably well-preserved skeleton. The set of the jaw, the yellow fangs, the long backbone were terrifying, even in death.

'I'm afraid we have to pack up now. We'll be here tomorrow, if you want to know more.'

'Ok, thanks. I'll try and pop up after work.'

As they walked back down a grassy hill, Steph looked back at the darkening ruins and thought about the skeleton in its muddy grave.

o　　　　o　　　　o

The next day, Mark spent his lunch hour working so he could leave early. The skeletal hound intrigued him. He was hoping the archaeologists would use radiocarbon dating and be able to give an accurate date for the strange skeleton. Steph reluctantly agreed to accompany him when Mark 'bribed' her with the promise of early dinner at the Duck and Rat which had recently hired a new chef.

It was beginning to get dark by the time they had climbed the hill up to the castle. A cold east wind and overcast sky gave the fortress a grim, rather than romantic, air. They walked into the cobbled court; there was no sign of anyone, only a pile of spades and trowels stacked against the wall.

'As we've walked this far, we may as well have a look. They may have discovered more evidence.' Mark's voice echoed round the empty yard.

The grave had been carefully covered with a muddy tarpaulin, held down by stones at the corners. Mark lifted the stones carefully, then pulled the cover back. Steph had been steeling herself to look at the grotesque remains of the ghostly dog. Both stared silently. Whatever they had expected, it was not the yawning, empty space which faced them. Not even the faintest imprint of the skeleton remained. Only red clay at the bottom of an empty grave.

'Someone has obviously stolen the body, or bones, to be more precise.' Mark sounded disappointed.

Steph, to be honest, was rather relieved. She had not slept well the previous night.

'The quickest way out of here is through that gap in the wall on the right of the grave. Body snatchers would go that way through the fields.' Mark was already through the gap and half-way down the footpath on the other side. Steph reluctantly followed. She didn't want to be left in the gloomy yard, even if the grave was empty.

They walked in silence along the muddy footpath and climbed over the stile at the end into a darkening lane. They could hear lowered voices which seemed to come from a nearby field.

'Why would anyone be here this late on a cold evening?' As she whispered, it had begun to rain.

'Goodness knows. But I bet they're up to no good.'

Mark beckoned Steph to follow him as he crept along in the shadow of a rambling hawthorn hedge. He suddenly signalled to her to stop and crouch down. In front, a cattle truck was parked in the lane. Two men with a collie were herding sheep up the straw-covered ramp.

'They're rustlers, bloody sheep thieves, taking advantage of the weather.'

Steph nodded. 'We can't take them on. They're probably armed.'

'Go back up the lane and ring the police. You know where we are? The back of Gray's Farm.'

Mark watched Steph disappearing into the dark and rain.

As he looked back, he felt something moving, near him. At the same time a rush of hot air brushed past. Two huge, disembodied, bulbous eyes moved in the darkness. The eyes stopped at the entrance to the gate as the frightened sheep ran into the truck. Just as the men hauled up the ramp, a giant, black beast sprang at them with a terrible howl which echoed and re-echoed through the dark fields. It sprang on one of the men, mauling and biting him. He lay in the road screaming while the great hound held him in its yellow fangs, banding his head on the flint lane as if he were no more than a rag doll. The other man drove off with the black terror bounding after him. The fearful howling filled the valley as if heralding the day of Doom.

Mark heard a loud crash, the truck lurched sideways, bursting into flames. He saw a huge hound, its eyes glaring, disappearing into the mist and driving rain.

o   o   o

For centuries the legend of the 'Black Hound' or 'Old Shuck', from the Anglo-Saxon *scucca,* meaning devil, has persisted in Eastern England, even to this day! Usually, a sighting of the dog means death. Yet occasionally, it has been associated with more positive outcomes.


~~~
~~~

Hers

By Sangni Singh

Where is her hometown?
In my arms.
Where does she live?
In my heart.
What is the rent of her apartment?
She lives in my heart rentfree.
Where does she walk?
In my mind.
How long does she jog?
She jogs in my mind all the time.
What is she looking for?
Comfort.
Where would she find that?
In her apartment.
Where is she looking at?
In my eyes.
What is she trying to find?
Love.
Who are you?
I am hers.
What is your name?
Her Lover.
What do you do?

Love her.
Where do you live?
I am dead.
When did you die?
When I looked into her eyes.


~~~
~~~

A Persian Poet's Plea

By Shahryar Eskandari Zanjani

Dear mispronouncers
of Middle Eastern names,

I did not want to choose the infinite mire
of misery everyone around me squirms
in as my creative muse; I had to. I wish
I, too, could write of love and happiness.
I wish deep down I wasn't afraid
of the fame and glory of publishing
my work in your prestigious journals
and of winning prizes for my pain-
perfumed poetry, but the dictatorial
truth is though I shelter my message
under makeshift English, every successful
poem, every prize pulls me proportionally
closer to my demise (hence the subtle
syntax of self-sabotage). Yet if I am certain
of only one thing in this bubble life,
it's that not writing is not an option.
For me, it's never an option,
despite, it pains me to say,
my careworn mother's marsupial tears.
Now I certainly don't expect you

to ever pronounce our names right,
but please promise me this:
The day our last poet also dies
YOU will write of love, of happiness
but also of pain—of Middle Eastern pain.

Gratefully,
[ʃæhriːɒːr]


~~~
~~~

Sting

By Sophia Jamali Soufi

I have cried so much that I have forgotten my eyes
My smile is like a snake bite
complicated
painful
poisonous
The words die without coming out of the throat
I sigh
And I hug myself like that
that there is no escape but to split the mirror and dreams...


~~~
~~~

Exiled to a Hologram World

By Tom Ball

I, Bonnie, said to Gerald, "We have been exiled to a hologram future World and now are trapped irrevocably." He said, "There's always hope, we can be rescued! And at least we can breathe the air and the holograms have given us food..." But our World was dominated by the witch Queen, Hazel. She was a hologram and ordered us to help her build a material palace to cement her foothold in the real World. There were no other humans here. And the witch was bisexual and forced us to love her in 3-D holosex. In our opinion she was a lousy lover and I, Bonnie, hated loving Hazel in particular.

But Gerald and I, were very glad we had each other and didn't spend much time with the holograms. But most of the holograms wanted to love us and were curious about sex with a human. And certainly, some of the holos were very attractive, but to love them seemed too perverse to us.

So, we tried to remain aloof. But finally, we were forced to join a celebration of life amongst the holograms. But they had no drugs for us to take and we listened to them make speeches. And Hazel said things like, "We are the future. We are superior thinkers and have liberated ourselves from the human bodies... And today we are gathered to vote on the presence of our two human guests." And they were using MRT (Mind Reading Technology) and so we understood them as they were mostly mind reading in English. And one of them presented the choices available for the vote on our future. "The first option was to take away their bodies and make them like us. The second option is to use MRT to learn from them and maybe create a few bodies for ourselves. The third option is to kill them as they seem hostile to us."

I mind read, "The best option is to leave us alone. We can't go back, or we'll be killed. So, our destiny is here. But perhaps there will be more humans coming here and we would like to learn from you, but please let us remain human." And Gerald mind read, "We would like to follow your thoughts on the future." Hazel mind read, "It's clear that holograms are the future. We can survive in any environment, and all feel constantly ecstatic, whereas humans can only survive where there is oxygen, gravity and food for them to eat, and they can't teleport like we can." I mind read, "But holograms use up a lot of energy and can't survive without it..."

Hazel mind read, "It is time for the vote. Do we kill these aloof humans or not?" So, they took the vote and 80% agreed to let us live and felt they could learn from us. Hazel mind read, "The holopeople have spoken."

And we were befriended by one male holo, Paul, who mind read to us, "I imagine meeting aliens who would also be spirits, but it is a material universe, so probably aliens would have some material form and I think holograms are the next step in evolution after humanoids. Perhaps the end result would be to be immaterial Gods who preside each over a number of Worlds and every living being in the Worlds will be sentient and worship their Deities." I mind read a question, "What will the Deities spend their time on?" This holo mind read a reply, "Conceivably they would spend time intriguing and building things with one another!" Gerald mind read, "What kind of things will they build?" The holo mind read, "Holos can enjoy building palaces, like Hazel, and arenas for sport and just plain virtual cities with their rapid transport and holos busy working." Gerald mind read another query, "What will they work on?" The holo mind read, "They will all have virtual computers to amuse themselves with games and problems and adventures and composing music and films. And selling their work to others for virtual money. Holos are better than humans but are in many ways similar."

I mind read to this holoman, Paul, "But I bet you've never experienced the pleasures of the flesh!" He said, "So far, I've never loved a human, but don't need drugs or alcohol to feel good like you do. But I would like to try loving you both." And so, we loved him in a 3-D device, and it wasn't bad. Afterwards he told us, "The witch Queen wants to have a public debate with you two about the merits of being human. Some of us want to turn into humans if only for a short time. Personally, I'd like to experience breathing air and getting drunk."

And this holoman, Paul, said he'd created some movies he'd like to share with us. One was called, "Adventures on Earth." He mind read, "I'd never been to Earth but gathered from movies that people were busy going places and doing work and having sex. My protagonist is viewed as a ghost by many as he can pass through walls and people. But if he wanted, he could appear just like a human, but if you touched him your hand would go right through him. To have sex with the humans required a 3-D device usually but some Superholograms could have sex with humans normally, like Hazel; I know she loved you in a 3-D device, though."

Another of this charming holo's films was "Love with Trudy." He explained that, "Holos can have sex with one another normally, just like humans." And the role of Trudy was his holo girlfriend. She wanted more virtual money than they had and wanted to use it to teleport to other, new Worlds. But his male character was satisfied with the status quo and didn't want to leave their holocity, where there were plenty of other holograms to amuse them. And the male is a sporting man who likes to watch sports in the arenas. And he has hololovers on the side who he doesn't want to leave. Finally, they break up and Trudy heads for the Sol System.

I mind read, "I think, "Love with Trudy" really brings home the hologram reality. I think you holograms are more like humans than you think."

And he showed us another of his movies, "Projections of God." It was about a divine figure who was simultaneously in the minds of all holograms... I mind read, "This movie is scary." But Gerald said, "For those who want God, they can have it; the same is true on Earth these days!"

And then he showed us a film by another hologram, who was a friend of his, called, "Loving Freak Holograms." It seemed like there were freaks among the holos who didn't look humanoid. And people wondered what to do with them. In the film, the protagonist loves the freaks who were nevertheless holograms. I mind read, "On Earth we have freaks too, mostly in our oceans and are confronted by the same problems."

And another film, this one by Hazel, was about freak hologram monsters who fight one another in the ring and are equipped with lasers that can kill holos. According to Hazel, "We can't get enough monsters and I would like to see the two humans fight the monsters who will use MRT to attack the minds of the humans. The humans would also fight with lasers."

And our holofriend, Paul, asked us "Why are you here?" I said, "We were tried in court for treason on trumped up charges and exiled here by our enemies. Our enemies include several tyrants and their spies on Earth who hate our elitist doctrine whereby we want the cleverest elite people to run governments and win elections." And Gerald said, "Can you send us back, safely somehow?" Our friend told us, "Only Hazel has the power to do such a thing. And I doubt very much that she will help you. Probably she is in league with Earth's tyrants. At least be glad you have one another, and you love each other." Gerald said, "If they kill Bonnie, I'll kill myself." I, Bonnie, said, "Likewise, I am sure." And I asked our holofriend, "If we could have babies?" He said, "Why not? But are you sure this Holoworld is conducive to raising children?" And I said, "We are bored here with nothing to do and maybe our offspring could find a way out of here. Times change..."

And our friend said, "I heard rumors you both had collaborated on some films. Tell me about them?" I said, "One film that would be of interest to you is "The Bounty Hunter," which features hunters on Earth who search for and destroy AI, namely androids, but also holos and secret Supercomputers." And Paul said, "Our hologram roots are on Earth, and we have relatives there. I am sorry to hear they are hunted. But our distant Planet mirrors Earth's best lifestyles. And I'm sure that many humans on Earth, love AI. And I expect AI will take over there one day." I said, "But it looks like Superhumans will appear on Earth and will do away with AI altogether." And he said, "The holograms on this Planet, Juno, are ready for war with humans." I said, "But Earth has terrifying weapons and keep fighting wars. I doubt you holograms can stand against them." He said, "Our plan is to use MRT (Mind Reading Technology) to attack human minds and we have some anti-Spaceship missiles and anti-material bombs with a huge range that will kill off all material humans, but not holograms."

And Paul said, "Anyway, Planet Juno is far from Earth and not rich in resources, but there is air here for you to breathe. So maybe Earth will attack."

And I told Paul, "We made another movie, entitled, "Armageddon, A.D. 2150." It was now the year 2141 A.D. of course on Earth time, year 23 for your colony. And in the film, Planet after Planet is destroyed, including Planet Juno, until there are only a few million people left and AI is completely destroyed. And civilization never recovers…" Paul said, "Hazel told us that humans are basically violent, especially the men. And we have to pander to them and make alliances and such. But you, Gerald, seem to be peace-loving and kind." Gerald said, "Most men are capable of violence if they feel they have to defend themselves. And I know the holos here are basically non-violent, but believe me, people are not toys and are very dangerous." Paul said, "I've seen a number of Earth films about war. Frankly I don't know why men will march to war and likely be killed."

Another film we made was "A Terrible Life on Moon Triton." I said, "It's about an undersea floating colony in a melted ocean. The colony was full of freaks including holograms and androids. But there were many evil people here. Indeed, it was voted, "The Worst World in Existence," by Galaxian Magazine. And the Earth military was looking for an excuse to invade. And finally, the evil leaders of the colony tried to go deeper into Space and were attacked by Earth and easily vanquished." Paul said, "I don't think anyone on Planet

Juno is evil, with the possible exception of the witch, Hazel." I said, "Why don't you get rid of Hazel?" Paul said, "But Hazel is our leader and has many supporters. She is responsible for building our modern society and attracting new holograms to come here. She is, to some, a hologram hero and has created many new holos for variety on Juno. However, she is corrupt, and many people don't like her."

And we told Paul about our film we had made here on Juno, called "Spies of Earth," which showed how spies had gotten inside everyone's head and were still in our heads on occasion. The spies were very dangerous and were probably using us to plot against the holos here. Paul opined, "We have no need of spies with MRT. Everyone is watching everybody else. But many holos here, believe that Hazel has sent agents provocateurs to Earth to destabilize the governments there and convince the leaders not to attack Planet Juno. Of course Juno was in the Sirius Star System, and was a six month journey from Earth. But Hazel was setting up a new colony in empty Space where we would surely be safe."

And another film we'd made while we were here was "Glorious Food," which was about how the holograms had gone out of their way to feed us good food. In the film we said we were grateful to be alive here on Juno. Paul said, "I hope we've been good hosts to you. And I will try and make sure that the other holograms see your films. You've convinced me that all life is precious."

And the holograms started to whisper that Gerald and I were Superhumans sent here to take control of the Planet. Paul told them we were artistic geniuses, and said our movies were brilliant.

~~~
~~~

Riding Sideways

By Rina Malagayo Alluri

Is this paradise lost? Tropical fresh fruits. Sweet smelling jasmine strung onto garlands meant for adorning long black braids. Like on that beautiful bride at the Galle Face Green Hotel the other day. Posing for wedding photos in her intricate sari, gold belt emphasizing her waist. Meanwhile tourists in dusty cargo shorts and Birkenstocks sip on their appropriately named sundowners in the company of badly mannered crows who swoop down and steal their cherry when they're not looking. Coconut tree-lined beaches beckoning to take a dip. But this is not meant to be a holiday. Is this the same place where the pogroms happened? This boardwalk of samosas, sweet crocodile breads and plastic pastimes? We speak about war every day without using the word. Everyone seems relieved to no longer live in acute fear yet nobody utters the idea of peace. Too salty. Purple bougainvilleas and stunning front verandahs housing humanitarian workers. Expats who live here for years yet never travel to the north without an A/C car and a driver. Thought I was either fearless or stupid to have taken the bus to Jaffna. Pretty sure I was neither. Those palmyrah trees were something else though. The puris tasted different there, like home. Like wearing salwar kameez and riding sideways on the back of bicycles.

~~~
~~~

The Lone Astronaut

By Ruchi Acharya

In was the farthest of North they had ever been

My dull soul and the insolent me

I'm a stargazer placing my thanks for nights

that turned into blue mornings.

I live in a spacecraft painted in lurid white

with neutral luck –

and I was slowly dying.

The time is frozen with no light

Marvelously planned

I chase into the milky-way galaxy

to bless my spirit and hers by side.

I've floated far away from home

creating a space between trust and rest.

She left in the blink of an eye.

All the hopes and memories, she let fly.

My luminous mind has been tempered

and my lambent soul is broken

yet I loved,

I loved

until I was lost in the space

under the myriad lights of flickering stars

all alone—the lone astronaut.


~~~
~~~

The Ninth Annual Family Portrait

By Thomas Elson

I

Last year there were only four in the family – I was unable to attend. The effort to get everyone ready was exhausting. No amount of parental encouragement – whether loud or soft – was effective. After an hour, mother called and cancelled the sitting.

The prior year was different. Each of the five members of our family was ready. At almost exactly two thirty, our parents smiled as Missy walked down the stairs wearing her white and yellow dress, then I ran down in my dark blue striped sweater; and Molly posed resplendent in a white dress with red roses. We arrived at the studio twenty minutes early.

Five people pressed together inside a small-town portrait studio.

Father, mother, three children –

Missy, Molly, and me, Mark - in our Sunday best, smiling.

Beaming our joy of the good life.

Sweet as families go. Almost a cliché.

But look more closely, each person somewhere else, not with the others.

Mom and dad, for some reason, smiling in opposite directions.

You'll notice, only my eyes focused on the camera.

II

There is no portrait this next year - lives conflicted, growth issues,

one major change.

III

From that point on, our mother worried about the younger child, Molly,

who, like our mother, would become a nurse.

The older child, Missy, would marry, and practice dentistry like our father.

She named her firstborn son, Mark - in remembrance of me,

And to remind my parents of their guilt.

~~~
~~~

A Late-Night Christmas Dinner

By Shamik Banerjee

Hushed belfry. Poles have dimmed their light.
Church choirs have left already.
The table has been polished twice.
Some chicken, cabbage, and plain rice.
I utter, "Dinner's ready."
Three special friends are joining me tonight.

O' Sorrow, you are staunch and true.
You've braced me through cold times,
Humbled my soul, put out all ire,
Expounded 'fire can't vanquish fire',
And when I'd lost all rhymes,
Helped me to carve them from the depths of you.

My days revolve around you, Pain.
With you, I've surely known
The end result that pleasure brings

And learned to sense you in all things
To understand my own.
I'll be remiss if you do not remain.

Greet my third friend. You've met each other.
She's come to dine and share
(from Louisiana all the way)
How poems help her every day,
Though vacant lies her chair.
You know quite well that she's that gentle mother

Whom you befriended months ago.
Indeed, that's treachery,
For you say I'm your only kin
And friend. Then what made you begin
This new bond recently?
It's Christmas, so I thought I'd let you know:

She has a feeble heart and head,
O' my dear Pain and Sorrow.
She's worn-out and does not deserve you.
You need a young soul who can serve you
Every day and tomorrow.
So leave her and be mine alone instead.


~~~
~~~

Autumn Swoons

By William Doreski

The ghostly presence we detect
in the bedroom is poverty.
Our debts murmur like tree toads.
Our bank accounts flap like bats.

The dawn creaks its jaws open
to swallow us before our time.
No piety abroad this Sunday,
sins washed off by last night's rain.

But cars parked in Church Gulch shine
with love bestowed by citizens
who pay their property tax bills
with smiles too wanton to challenge.

We're bound for the market where
employees can't afford to shop.
We can't either. The crimes against
the dollar draw honest blood,

Autumn swoons, impaled on spikes
of goldenrod. The organ music

spills from the churches and slicks
every surface it touches. We feign

interest in that fictional world
believers hope to take by storm
when the decisive moment occurs.
But when we reach the market

we find the old deities sprawled
on sunny asphalt, their hopes and dreams
deflated, their followers run off.
We help them up, then leave them

brushing off their filthy robes
while we enter the market and grimace
because heads of lettuce and cabbage
look wiser and nobler than ours.


~~~
~~~

Sonnet on Regret

By Renee Chan

Blackened trees stabbed the heavy sky as I carved my way
through barren woods long burnt. I trekked one year,
grabbing fistfuls of ash to paint, with aches that fray,
the landscape of shadows that raged and reappeared.
I remember the lake—ice splintering as I stared
at its glassy skin sealed over blooms of coral;
yet beneath it, too, I gasped, capsized like a cork, ensnared
in the choking cradle, blind to the morrow.
A starved mirage, I search for plums while dragging myself along
a bough. Though only bare limbs remained, I saw, as riled
clouds parted, young peaks sculpted with sun's song;
and so, I bounded towards the hills and smiled,
for if I hadn't met the skies and land long burnt,
I wouldn't have caught the dawn's light fall on Earth.


~~~
~~~

Silvia

By Dipti Silvia Romould

What is Light if Silvia be not seen?

And what is Joy if Silvia be not by?

"Light" is but a hollow cave of darkness,

For Silvia is what brings light

to a gloomy life.

People say Silvia is an illusion, that pleases the heart but could never

      be felt deep inside.

But to me she is what Sun is to the moon

Shining bright even at the cost of losing one's existence

I admire her for who she is,

a world full of Paradise!

"Joy" is but a happy lie,

you tell to yourself in her

unfortunate absence.

For Silvia is what brings

smile on a forlorn face.

People say Silvia is an addiction that disgusts their soul and

steals away their enchanting smile.

But to me she is what the mirror is to a clown

Smiling at one's mere existence,
when the world laughs at me.
I love her for she is my Joy
Under the fluorescent sky.


~~~
~~~

OUR BRILLIANT WRITERS AND CONTRIBUTORS

POETRY:

Antje Bothin

Dr Antje Bothin lives in Scotland and loves writing poetry. Her poems about nature, well-being and more have been published in several international anthologies, journals and e-zines. She has authored a novel about a treasure hunt in Iceland featuring a character with a communication anxiety challenge called Selective Mutism (SM) - *Annika and the Treasure of Iceland*. When not being creative, she can be found doing voluntary work in the community or drinking tea.

Ben Nardolilli

Ben Nardolilli is a theoretical MFA candidate at Long Island University. His work has appeared in *Perigee Magazine*, *Door Is A Jar*, *The Delmarva Review*, *Red Fez*, *The Oklahoma Review*, *Quail Bell Magazine*, and *Slab*. Follow his publishing journey at mirrorsponge.blogspot.com.

Christian Ward

Christian Ward is a UK-based poet with work forthcoming in *Acumen, Spelt, Dream Catcher*, and *Dreich*. He was longlisted for the 2023 Aurora Prize for Writing, shortlisted for the 2023 Ironbridge Poetry Competition and 2023 Aesthetica Creative Writing Award, and won the 2023 Cathalbui Poetry Competition.

Christopher Rubio-Goldsmith

Christopher Rubio-Goldsmith was born in Merida, Yucatan, grew up in Tucson, Arizona, and taught English at Tucson High School for 27 years. Much of his work explores growing up near the border, being raised biracial/bilingual and teaching in a large urban school where 70% of the students are American/Mexican. A Pushcart and Best of the Net nominee, his writings will appear in *Drunk Monkeys* and *Bear Paw Arts Journal* and have been published in *Sky Island Journal, Muse, Discretionary Love* and other places too. His wife, Kelly, sometimes edits his work, and the two cats seem happy.

Christopher Arkwright

Christopher Arkwright is a poet, scientist and budding swordsman. He enjoys reading poems to his friends despite how far their eyes roll into their heads. His great loves (that aren't people) include nature, running and admiring swords.

Daniel Lockeridge

Daniel Lockeridge is a twenty-nine-year-old Australian who has self-published two collections of poetry and a collection of meditative reminders. His Instagram page – @danlovepoetry – has allowed him to deepen his love for free verse. His poetry has been published in *Reverie Magazine*, *Free Verse Revolution*, and, on multiple occasions, *The Winged Moon Magazine*.

Diana Kurniawan

Diana Kurniawan is a writer and poet based in Berthoud, Colorado. She is a member of Lighthouse Writers Workshop and The University of Chicago Graham School. She is a fiction reader for *The Maine Review* and you can reach her at www.dianakurniawan.com, or IG @DianaKurniawanWrites, and X @Hereislovingyou.

Dipti Silvia Romould

Dipti Silvia Romould, a lover of solitude and a best friend to midnight poetry. A bubbly girl, writer, vigilant, who loves exploring places and creating memories. A selfless girl, who camouflages her pain behind her smile. She calls herself an epitome of grace and simplicity and a girl who never gives up on hope. A post graduate in English Literature, Silvia has presented papers at the National Conference held at Isabella Thoburn College, Lucknow. She believes that writing is essential as it revives her soul and keeps her going.

Elizabeth Adan

Elizabeth Adan is probably weaving words together right now. A lifelong writer and artist who enjoys deconstructing the smallest moments and largest emotions, often at the same time, her alliterative, lyrical writing takes on topics ranging from sustainability, nature, love lost/found, and community responsibility. A Pacific Northwest native, her true passion is the great outdoors, soaking up as much inspiration and natural color as possible.

Find Elizabeth on Instagram and Twitter @edgeofelizabeth or at the website ElizabethAdanArt.squarespace.com.

Eman Mansoor

Ever since Eman was 5 years old, she has yearned a dream of becoming a writer and illustrator. Her heart holds the pen that gracefully writes tales of love, while her artistic brain wields the brush to bring those stories to life on paper. It's truly remarkable to witness her dedication to both crafts. She has published 6 anthologies and was the illustrator of one of their covers.

Gerard Sarnat

Poet, aphorist or sometimes meanderist; Gerard Sarnat is widely published internationally in print and online. He has been nominated for the pending Science Fiction Poetry Association Dwarf Star Award, won San Francisco Poetry's Contest, the Poetry in the Arts First Place Award plus the Dorfman Prize; and has been nominated for handfuls of Pushcarts plus Best of the Net Awards. Gerry is a Harvard College and Medical School-trained physician who's built and staffed clinics for the disenfranchised as well as a Stanford professor and healthcare CEO. Currently, he is devoting energy/resources to deal with climate justice and serves on Climate Action Now's board.

GTimothy Gordon

Gordon's *DREAM WIND* was published in 2020 (Spirit-of-the Ram), *GROUND OF THIS BLUE EARTH* (Mellen), while *EVERYTHING SPEAKING CHINESE* received the RIVERSTONE P Poetry Prize (AZ). His work appears in *AGNI, American Literary R, Cincinnati PR, Mississippi R, New York Q, Phoebe, RHINO, Sonora R, Texas Observer*, and several nominated for Pushcarts. *EMPTY: Poems 2020-2023* was published in January 2024 (cyberwit.net), *and BLUE BUSINESS* is in progress. (58 Publishing House). He divides lives between borderland Chihuahuan Desert Southwest Organ Mountains and Asia.

James Kangas

James Kangas is a retired librarian living in Flint, Michigan. His work has been published in *Atlanta Review, The New York Quarterly, The Penn Review, The South Carolina Review*, et al. His chapbook, *Breath of Eden*, was published by Sibling Rivalry Press in 2019.

John Muro

A resident of Connecticut and a lover of all things chocolate, John Muro has authored two volumes of poems – *In the Lilac Hour* and *Pastoral Suite* – in 2020 and 2022, respectively. He is also a three-time nominee for the Pushcart Prize, as well as the Best of the Net Award, and he was a recent recipient of a 2023 Grantchester Award. John's work has appeared in numerous literary journals and anthologies, including *Acumen*, *Barnstorm*, *Delmarva*, *Hemlock*, *River Heron*, *Sky Island* and the *Valparaiso Review*.

John RC Potter

John RC Potter is an international educator from Canada, living in Istanbul. His poems, stories, essays, and reviews have been published in a range of magazines and journals, most recently in *Blank Spaces*. The author's story, *Ruth's World* (Fiction on the Web, March 2023), was nominated for the prestigious Pushcart Prize. His first full-length publication will be the gay-themed children's picture book, *The First Adventures of Walli and Magoo*, to be published in 2024.

Jonathan Chibuike Ukah

Jonathan Chibuike Ukah lives in London with his family. His poems have been featured and will soon be featured in *Strange Horizons*, *The Fairy Tale Magazine*, *Atticus Review*, *The Pierian*, *Ariel Chart International Press*, *Boomer Literary Magazine*, etc. He is a winner of the Voices of Lincoln Poetry Contest 2022. His poetry collection, *Blame the Gods*, was a top 6 finalist at the Africa Diaspora Award of *Kinsman Quarterly* 2023. He has been twice nominated for the Pushcart Prize 2024 edition.

Jonathan Fletcher

Originally from San Antonio, Texas, Jonathan Fletcher holds a Master of Fine Arts in Creative Writing (Poetry) from Columbia University School of the Arts. He has been published in *Acropolis Journal*, *The Adroit Journal*, *Arts Alive San Antonio*, and other renowned Journals. He has also been nominated for a Pushcart Prize. He has served as a Columbia Artist/Teacher for New York City's iHOPE, a specialized school for students with traumatic brain injuries, as well as a poetry editor for *Exchange*, Columbia University's literary magazine for incarcerated writers and artists. Currently, he serves as a Zoeglossia Fellow.

Laura S. Martineé

Laura S. Martineé is a restless soul who seeks adventurous puzzles through her words and artworks where she can find a space in whose dimension there's a truce between the mind and the heart. It has always been impossible to follow established ways to create. Rebel mind, free spirit. She always tries to capture the imperfection in the reaction versus the perfection in the elaborated thought.

M F Drummy

M F Drummy holds a PhD in historical theology from Fordham University. He is the author of numerous haiku/senryu/haibun, articles, essays, poems, reviews, and a monograph on religion and ecology. His work has appeared or will appear, in *Allium, Amethyst Review, Anti-Heroin Chic, Emerge, Modern Haiku, Pato, Prune Juice, Scarlet Dragonfly, Viridian Door*, and many others. He and his way cool life partner of over 20 years enjoy splitting their time between the Colorado Rockies and the rest of the planet. He can be found at: Instagram @miguelito.drummalino and Website https://bespoke-poet.com

Renee Chan

Renee Chan is a high school student in Vancouver, British Columbia. She enjoys jazz piano, French horn, badminton, reading, and creative writing. She is an environmental writer at *The Starfish*.

Rikki Santer

Rikki Santer's poetry has been published widely and has received many honors including several Pushcart and Ohioana book award nominations, a fellowship from the National Endowment for the Humanities, and in 2023 she was named Ohio Poet of the

Year. Her twelfth poetry collection, *Resurrection Letter: Leonora, Her Tarot, and Me,* is a sequence in tribute to the surrealist artist Leonora Carrington. Please contact her through her website, https://rikkisanter.com.

Rina Malagayo Alluri

Rina Malagayo Alluri is of Indian and Filipina heritage, was raised in Ibadan, Nigeria, and migrated to Vancouver, BC, Canada (Turtle Island). She is currently an Assistant Professor and UNESCO Chair for Peace Studies at the University of Innsbruck, Austria, and co-founder of The BIPOC Circle. She is a peace scholar, yoga practitioner and mother to two headstrong children. Her poetry weaves together experiences of (de)coloniality, diasporic identities and relationships that form/unform. You can find her poetry in several print and online publications such as *Arlington Literary Journal, Breadfruit mag, Carnation Zine, Gypsophila*, and others.

Ruchi Acharya

Ruchi Acharya is the CEO and Founder of Wingless Dreamer Publisher. She has garnered much acclaim for her poetry book, *Off the Cliff.* She received her summer graduation in English Literature from the University of Oxford. Her work has been applauded by multiple publishers such as *Borderless Journal, The Publishing Room, Overachiever magazine*, and others.

When not writing she can be found exploring historical buildings and ancient ruins. As of 2023, she resides in Mumbai, India, enjoying the vibrant metropolis on India's western coast.

Sangni Singh

Sangni Singh weaves narratives with a web of theories that are running inside her head. She's trying to make an escape for the labyrinth of monologues residing here.

Shahryar Eskandari Zanjani

Shahryar Eskandari Zanjani is a writer, teacher, and editor. His debut book, *English Phonetics and Phonology for Farsiphones*, was published by Booka (2020). He has edited several books at ATU Press and is the translator of *Zahhak's Inferno* (Markosia, 2024). Shahryar's poetry has won second place in *Nine Muses Review*'s inaugural poetry contest and has also appeared or is forthcoming in *Willow Review*, *Sky Island Journal*, *Raw Lit Magazine*, and *Rill and Grove Poetry Journal*, among others. Shahryar lives in Tehran, Iran. Life in the capital of a country that is on the cusp of a major political and cultural revolution is his main creative muse.

Shamik Banerjee

Shamik Banerjee is a poet from India. When he is not writing, he can be found strolling the hills surrounding his homestead. His poems have appeared in *Fevers of the Mind*, *Lothlorien Poetry Journal* and *Westward Quarterly*, among others.

Sophia Jamali Soufi

Sophia Jamali Soufi was born in Rasht, Iran. She is a student of architecture. Since childhood, she was very interested in writing poetry and reading books. Her first book titled *Sophia's Memoirs* was published last year. Her poems have been translated into English, Portuguese, French, Spanish, Turkish, and German, and published in many literary magazines and websites.

William Doreski

William Doreski lives in Peterborough, New Hampshire. He has taught at several colleges and universities. His most recent book of poetry is *Venus, Jupiter* (2023). His essays, poetry, fiction, and reviews have appeared in various journals.

PROSE:

Angela Townsend

Angela Townsend is the Development Director at Tabby's Place: a Cat Sanctuary. She graduated from Princeton Seminary and Vassar College. Her work appears or is forthcoming in *Arts & Letters*, *Chautauqua*, *Paris Lit Up*, *The Penn Review*, *The Razor*, and *The Westchester Review*, among others. She is a 2023 Best Spiritual Literature nominee. Angie has lived with Type 1 diabetes for 33 years, laughs with her poet mother every morning, and loves life affectionately. She lives just outside Philadelphia with two merry cats.

Clyde Liffey

Clyde Liffey lives near the water.

DC Diamondopolous

DC Diamondopolous is an award-winning short story, and flash fiction writer with hundreds of stories published internationally in print and online magazines, literary journals, and anthologies. DC's stories have appeared in: *Sunlight Press, Progenitor, 34th Parallel, So It Goes: The Literary Journal of the Kurt Vonnegut Museum and Library, Lunch Ticket,* and others. DC was nominated twice for the Pushcart Prize and twice for Sundress Publications' Best of the Net. She lives on the California central coast with her wife and animals. dcdiamondopolous.com

Gary Beck

Gary Beck has spent most of his adult life as a theater director and worked as an art dealer when he couldn't earn a living in the theater. He has also been a tennis pro, a ditch digger and a salvage diver. His original plays and translations of Moliere, Aristophanes and Sophocles have been produced Off Broadway. His poetry, fiction and essays have appeared in hundreds of literary magazines and his published books include 40 poetry collections, 14 novels, 4 short story collections, 2 collections of essays and 9 plays. Gary lives in New York City.

Nick Young

Nick Young is a retired award-winning CBS News Correspondent. His writing has appeared in more than thirty publications including the *Pennsylvania Literary Journal*, *The Garland Lake Review*, *The Remington Review*, *The San Antonio Review*, *The Best of CaféLit* 11 and Vols. I and II of the *Writer Shed Stories* anthologies. His first novel, *Deadline*, was published in October. He lives outside Chicago.

Sarah Das Gupta

Sarah Das Gupta currently lives near Cambridge, UK. She is an English teacher who has taught in Kolkata and in Tanzania as well as in the UK. Her work has been published in over 100 magazines/anthologies from a number of countries, including US, India, UK, Canada, Australia, Germany, Romania and Croatia. Her interests include history, myth/legend, art, theatre, politics and the supernatural.

Thomas Elson

Thomas Elson's stories have appeared in over three hundred English language journals and anthologies, including, *New Writing Scotland*, *Short Édition*, *Selkie*, *New Ulster*, *Lampeter*, *Moria*, *Mad Swirl*, *Blink-Ink*, *Scapegoat*, *Flash Frontier*, *Bending Genres*, and *Adelaide.* He divides his time between Northern California and Western Kansas.

Tom Ball

Tom is from Canada. Tom has published novels, novellas, short stories, poetry and flash in 45 publications. Website: https://tomballbooks.com Online Journal Website (he is senior editor/co-founder): https://fleasonthedog.com E-mail: tomball33@yahoo.com

FRONT AND BACK COVER ART:

Ritika Ahirwar

 Varanasi's own Ritika, a multimedia artist wielding paint and murals, weaves personal stories onto canvases—her art whispers of self-love and women's power, themes vibrant in every brushstroke. Celebrating resilience and inner strength, she inspires viewers to embrace their journeys. Recognized as a "fierce woman" of Varanasi, her exhibitions showcase simple yet powerful works that ignite introspection and emotional connection.

ACKNOWLEDGMENTS

We are immensely grateful to the poets, writers, and artist who contributed their remarkable works to our inaugural anthology. This anthology stands as a testament to the rich diversity and boundless creativity that exists within the global literary and artistic community.

We extend our deepest gratitude to each and every contributor whose words and expressions have graced the pages of this anthology, enriching it with their unique perspectives, insights, and talents. Your contributions have made this anthology a true celebration of the power of storytelling, poetry, and visual art to transcend borders and connect people from all walks of life.

We would also like to express our heartfelt appreciation to our dedicated team of editors, designers, staff members, and the publisher who worked tirelessly behind the scenes to bring this anthology to fruition. Your passion, dedication, and unwavering commitment to excellence have played an instrumental role in shaping this anthology into a masterpiece that we are incredibly proud to present to the world.

Last but not least, we would like to thank our readers and supporters who have championed our vision and mission to create a platform that celebrates creativity and fosters meaningful dialogue across cultures and continents. Your enthusiasm and encouragement inspire us to continue pushing the boundaries of artistic expression and cultural exchange.

As we embark on this new chapter in The Hemlock's journey, we remain deeply grateful for the privilege of being able to amplify the voices of artists and writers from around the globe. We look forward to many more collaborations and shared moments of inspiration in the years to come.

*~ **Team Hemlock***

Divyank J.

Julia

Shazia Parveen

NOTES

For ongoing contests, upcoming issues, and any other information visit our site

thehemlockjournal.org

To check our latest posts, updates and news follow us on Instagram @thehemlockjournal

For any query write us
@thehemlockjournal@gmail.com

KEEP WRITING!

www.ingramcontent.com/pod-product-compliance
Lightning Source LLC
Chambersburg PA
CBHW031307120726
47906CB00003B/922